I0654244

Model

Alisa Miller

Model

Alisa Miller

ISBN 978-1-84481-991-1

This book edition published 2010. - Model.

Published by New Line Publishing, 118 Gatley Road, Cheadle, Cheshire, SK8 4AD, UK.

Find us on the World Wide Web at: www.alisa-miller.com

Editing, cover and interior design by WebDirectStudio
www.webdirectstudio.com (website)
info@webdirectstudio.com (email)

Model

Alisa Miller

This e-book is sold subject to the condition that it shall not, by way of trade or otherwise, be lent, resold, hired out or otherwise circulated without the publisher's prior consent in any form of binding or cover other than that in which it is published and without a similar condition including this condition being imposed on the subsequent purchaser.

In modelling, there is no point in trying to prove you have a brain, so why even bother? I'd sooner save the energy for something more meaningful.

-Helena Christensen

Modelling killed me.

-Milla Jovovich

Acknowledgements

Every book, however the author might otherwise object, is the result of a collaborative effort. Model would not have happened had my agent not insisted, my publisher not supplied an editor equipped with endless patience and understanding and had not Lady Luck given me a partner I can really rely upon when I feel down, alone or miserable. To each of them I owe more than a mere 'thanks' can ever convey. A big thank you must also go to all my fans. Those whose daily interactions on Facebook, via email and through my website made me feel that I was doing something worthwhile, while my writing filled page after page. In many ways you help me be better than myself.

Introduction

There is something about writing fiction which is terrifying because it is, as an act, so liberating.

My non-fiction writing is easy to quantify because it is governed by a few simple rules: It has to be based on research and hard science and it has to help in some way.

Fiction, however, is not like that. When the idea first surfaced in a meeting I had with my agent it was 2009 and Winter and I was in an upmarket London department store having coffee with my agent.

I thought then that the idea sounded a little insane. I was not a novelist, I thought. I really wanted to help people.

My agent (whose name actually is Neil) patiently explained that fiction is more than just making up stories. In the verisimilitude of a fictional account we create a world which becomes a window for those who have not experienced it and through it we see a facet of life.

His explanation fascinated me enough to agree to the notion. Modelling was a large part of my life and modelling is a world and a career which is closed to most outside observers.

Inside its cliques and the 'circuit' models are commodities struggling to become big enough to call the shots.

The initial suggestion was for me to write about what I know and create a compelling storyline. I found this almost impossible to do without naming names and causing lawsuits so I struggled with the best way to tell a story which would capture something of the modelling world and also show how it works and how it affects those in it.

In the end I told, almost, my story. Not everything which I have detailed here happened to me but everything which I have detailed did happen.

Some of the characters I chose to portray are a mix of one or two people I know. The places are all real. The action did take place.

In writing this novel I discovered parts of my own self which I would not have discovered otherwise.

The book which became my break-out publication was (and is) *Ultimate Guide to the Perfect Relationship*. It was in Miami that I decided to finally leave the world of modelling and focus on writing instead.

I have, throughout this novel tried, perversely perhaps, to be as honest as possible, portraying facts and places and people as they really are.

I hope you have as much fun reading this book as I had writing it.

Alisa, Manchester, 2010

#1

Clare Studio, New York, NY.

The camera pans a little too low and the strobe flash blinds me and causes dark spots to shoot through the centre of my eyes.

"Great. Superb. Pout a little. Shoulders back. Now look smouldering." The creep behind the camera is going through the rote, his eye glued to the visor. That moment to him I am a paycheck and a means of getting his work out there. The guy aiming the fan which makes my hair fan and play in an imaginary wind is looking at my crotch where the black lace panties I am wearing allow, under the bright studio lights my skin to shine through. The stylist is blowing bubbles with her gum and is playing with a tendril of hair. She looks bored. She's seen it all before. She really is bored. The music playing in the background is failing to set the mood.

"Push your hips forward. Arch your back. Great"

Click. Click. Click. My eyes are starry from the bright flashes. My mind is on the plane I will be catching later this night. I arch my back knowing that my breasts then strain against the black lace bra. I am thinking just how to dodge the creep with the fan and get the guy with the camera to give me

Model

Alisa Miller

some stills for my portfolio without having to sleep with him.

It's then that I think just how great it is to be a model.

I am twenty-two years old and in a business which thrives on youth I am getting dangerously near retirement age. Laugh all you want but those power-hitters who still strut their staff on twenty-year-long careers get by on attitude which keeps their name in the press. They become brands for far more than modelling and this makes them bankable. They burn up though. More than just nights and days and sleep and sleeplessness.

This is hard to understand but what they burn up is a little bit of their soul.

Hard thing to do so here I am, worrying about retirement at twenty-two.

The gig is lingerie and the place is New York. MTV has become shorthand for a lifestyle and in this world models are like Gladiators. We have a short, glorious career.

I know the click-click-click of the camera as intimately as a runner hears the starting gun. It transforms me and I become more than just my flesh and bones and this is hard to really explain. Part of me comes alive when the camera clicks that is not there when I am not working. I feel it in my head and my chest and my heartbeat speeds up. My stomach muscles tighten flattening an already flat tummy, the tautness making the muscles I have worked so hard to build, suddenly thrum.

Model

Alisa Miller

This is a standard bread-and-butter job and yet, right now, for me it is so much more. I emote and I feel and suddenly I am alive, not just me, Alice but Alice the model which will make thousands of women pause and compare, imagine themselves in the lingerie and then, go out and buy, thinking that what I am wearing is the secret that will transform them too, make them get a new man or keep the one they have from straying.

I am Alice the model who will make thousands of men pause and look and secretly decide to buy their mistress a set of lingerie like the one I am wearing, hoping that when they see that on the secret woman in their lives they will see something of what I have projected into the image. The passion, the wanton, the wildness and the willingness, all rolled into one.

I know that thousand of prepubescent boys will find the catalogue in their parents' mail and go through it and I will become the one who took their innocence and broke them into the mysteries of wild, passionate, intense, no-strings-attached, no-barriers sex. I will then be the playmate of all those who tomorrow will grow up to become stockbrokers, bankers, shopkeepers and fathers. The backbone of our society, destined to find 'the one' have their 2.4 children and spend time pouring over expensive lingerie catalogues choosing underwear for their mistress.

We are all part of a chain of events which starts when we are not looking and goes on and on

Model

Alisa Miller

and on and I am part of it too, sometimes at the beginning and sometimes at a level that's too deep to even analyze.

You may think that models are too shallow or too preoccupied wit their looks to think like that but you'd be wrong. Beneath the superficial, polished surface where our hair and nails are the things which keep us together. Where the make up we wear and the eyeshadow we put on are looks which can transform us from angels to wanton demons, we think all the time. So many people are so preoccupied with how we look and how we photograph and how we walk and smile that we can switch off a little part of ourselves and look at everything from a distance and think. Think. Think.

And thinking does all the damage.

You don't want to be a model. You are never real. Each shot you take, no matter how thin you are and how hard you tried to diet and how much you sweated at the gym and felt the burn until the muscles beneath your skin rippled and moved with every movement, your body lithe, taut and wanted, will be photoshoped by some photographer's geek who knows more about fantasy women than real ones.

They will whiten your teeth and make your eyes luminous and slim down your arms and elongate your legs until what's there, in the magazine, the billboard and the poster is you and not you. When they get it right they capture the essence of what you are projecting. They capture the inner you, you're trying to put into the shoot. When they get it wrong you feel as if they have violated you from the inside out.

They've taken everything you have given them and twisted it, turning it into something else entirely and, in the process, fuelling an anorexic epidemic in teenage girls already under pressure to be not themselves but us. It's an unfair world. No one expects boys to be Olympic Athletes. Nor does anyone expect them to be millionaires. And yet they want their girlfriends to be like the models they see in magazines.

In the time between the clicks of the rapid-shooting camera I think about all this. I see myself as those around me see me. The guy with the camera is now excited. He has seen the spark and he's fallen under its spell so I know I am projecting right. The image in his viewfinder has already got a starring role in an orgy in his mind and, despite the air-conditioning and the fact that he is the one behind the bright lights and not in front of them, there is a slight sheen of sweat on his forehead.

He licks his tongue and his voice as he gives me encouragement and asks me to contort this way, look over there, pout, frown, smile seductively, is totally strained and I have him. I am working and it's working and I know that while he may want to sleep with me, right now, I can ask and he will give me everything I want in hope without demands.

I smile. I arch. I pout.

Model

Alisa Miller

"Alice, look over your right shoulder," he says and I comply. "Now look this way, straight at me."

He click-click-clicks and the creep with the fan senses that something has changed but does not know what. He looks uncertainly at me and then at his master and then back at me and I smile and the smile makes him blush and he tries hard now not to let it show that his eyes are undressing each almost-bare part of me.

"Perfect, that's the last batch." The photographer sounds exhausted and lets the camera dangle by his side. "We've got more than enough," he breathes like he's just ran the fastest mile ever.

"Tom," I am by his side, first name terms only ever with me. Personal rule I never break.

He turns to face me and his chest is rising and falling. "Can you give a flash card, some of the shots we did just now?" I ask before he has much time to think up his gameplan and right now the only thing he is really conscious of is that to say no is to close all the doors.

"It's over 2 Gigs" he says weakly.

"I have my own drive," I say, "I'll download them and give it back," and I smile and his eyes, never for an instant leaving mine agree before his mouth says yes, ok. Give me one moment. I thank him, on the spot, in front of the others like he's just done be the biggest favour in the world and he has become my best friend.

Model

Alisa Miller

***

Late, that night. It's the last flight out back to London and I am on the plane waiting for take off. My eyes are sore and I keep blinking to make sure that they do not get too dry and get inflamed. My body feels like I have ran a marathon and I am aware of every muscle ache as I move.

When you model you work. Your shoulders are always pushed back, your legs and arms are taut and posed. It's like ballet without the rapid motion. Try doing this for three hours solid and you begin to feel like it's breaking rocks.

I slump on my seat, jacket wrapped comfortingly around me, hiding my body. I had dressed down on purpose. I have this game which I play. I can become, according to how I dress a girl or a woman. The centre of attention or totally invisible. I had dressed not to be noticed, glad to be away from the lights and attention of the job, now just one soul amongst many, ready to command myself (in a way) to the fate decried by the gods and take to the skies in the plane that would take me back home.

On a plane, if you are a woman travelling alone you always pray you do not get some jerk on the make who will take the fact that mere chance has given us adjoining seats to be a sign from above that he will be in the running to score.

This time the gods did not hear my prayers. Had they heard me I might not have got so annoyed and I would have texted Ray as I did each time I got off my plane and then called him the moment I stepped into the terminal.

I didn't and I blame the jerk who sat next to me for that.

I no longer recall his name. He was one of those self-absorbed male primadonnas who think that the only reason a girl will not sleep with them is because she is a lesbian.

I take pains to blend and not attract attention when I am not working but modelling is a funny thing. You can hide but not if they have seen your picture on a billboard or a catalogue.

"You must be a movie star," was his opening conversational gambit upon sitting down next to me. He wore a pinstripe shirt, which I hate, and red suspenders which I deplore and he had take his suit jacket off.

I was trapped.

I spent the rest of the trans-Atlantic flight fighting off his attempts at familiarity and his entreaties to get my number. He was the kind who did not take no as a final answer. The kind I had learnt to never be found alone with at after-photoshoot parties and modelling agency parties. More than once I had had to console friends who had trusted fate and drink and had made the mistake in believing that men were gentlemen simply because they earnt a lot of money.

Take it from me. A model will not cry rape unless she wants to bring her career to an end, but the number of times we give in to unwanted sex as the lesser of two evils makes you wonder sometimes if there is any kind of human decency left in the world.

I had worn jeans on purpose and a sweater over them and I could see him itemising me, excited that he had suddenly a model at his side who had no choice but stay there. He was so sure that I would be a sure thing he could not wait to tell me about the high-end car he drove, the high-powered job he had and the massive bonuses he earnt.

His chatter got so much on my nerves that I was off the plane faster than I normally would, left my cell phone in my pocket, switched off and did not think about calling Ray until I had cleared customs and was on my way home.

It occurred to me then that I might as well surprise him. Crawl gratefully into his arms and smell the scent of him as he hugged me and then, after I had felt him fill the void in me and made the boor I had shared the flight with a distant memory, I would drift off with him, feeling safe.

It is raining in London. Nothing new. I watch the rain in the Black Cab's headlights, the red tail-lights of traffic as we head for Holland Park and the place I call home and I feel that I am back where I belong. Home where I know the rules and speak the language and I feel ok with the weather. In the morning I know I will have to call my agent and see what other gigs I am booked in for and go and spend at least an hour with my Pilates instructor and finish the day with 20 lengths of the pool and some press ups.

But that is hours away and right now, as I am in that Black Cab, all I can think is Ray. Tomorrow, I promise myself I must also call Cherisse and see if I can go with her to the tattoo removal clinic.

The thought makes me smile. I have known Cherisse for two years now and we have become close friends. Half French, half Italian and all British she lives above Ray and me and paints nude portraits for a living for outrageous sums of money. It helps that she paints her clients naked herself, to remove any last remaining traces of inhibition, as she says.

Ray and I have often giggled together trying to imagine her working. Cherisse has the kind of figure most models would kill for and despite being an avowed lover of Italian food she manages to maintain it with an ease which makes me green with envy sometimes.

I imagine how, after Ray has gone to work in the morning, I will give her a call, discuss the clinic. Cherisse had a barbed wire tattoo placed round her ankle and then found that it ruined more relationships than it made. The time had come for it to go, as she'd said herself.

The Black Cab pulls outside and I pay the driver on autopilot almost. He is obliging and comes round, helps me get my suitcase off the back.

The rain feels soft, refreshing, cold and in that weird way which comes with trans-Atlantic journeys I feel as I am dispossessed, split from myself so that I watch from across the street as I struggle with the suitcase wheels, getting them to obey the direction of my pull.

The doorman to our block of flats (yep, it is that kind of posy place) rushes to open the door for me, says hello with a smile even though it's 2.30am and I feel so happy suddenly that I am back in England that the effort of keeping my focus in New York and the horrible flight over suddenly wash off me and I feel rejuvenated.

I take the elevator, shaking the rain out of my hair and I am already dreaming of Ray's strong arms. The feel of his chest. His back as I run my hands over it.

The key slides silently into the lock and I am home.

I let go of my suitcase. Take my shoes off. Pad silently towards the bedroom and its semi-open door.

Ray's back is rippling hard, as attractive as I remember it. In the orange half-light that comes in the room from the sodium streetlights outside he appears like a demi-god. All angles and chiselled body parts. His head is thrown back, back arched, hips pressed into the bed.

I blink.

It's like I am someone else. A watcher intruding in my own life. I see myself standing silently by the bedroom door. Keys still clasped in one hand. In my socks. Hair tousled, slightly wet.

Ray's back muscles rippling hard.

I gasp. My breath catches in my throat Chest tightening.

Female legs clasp round his waist as he pumps. His breathing coming hard, like an athlete sprinting. And female cries being wrung, in unison to each thrust.

I recognise the voice long before I can see the barbed wire tattoo in the flickering light snaking round Cherisse's right ankle.

I step back. I knock a vase over with a crash. And I break. I run. I put my shoes on fast. Pull open the door and let it slam shut vaguely aware of a cry behind me. A male voice saying something urgent.

I do not stop. I cannot wait. The lift is not where it should be and I take the stairs two at a time, running down the service steps, blind to everything except the cry I can feel wrenching inside my chest and the pain of awareness that comes with the realisation of just how stupid I have been. And then I am at the foyer again and the doorman is surprised to see me and his surprise only makes the pain worse.

I move faster than he can react. Reaching the door, opening it, stepping out. I run blindly into the night then. Unaware of where I am heading. Feeling only the fact that there is nothing left to feel any more and the wetness of the sky, the rain around me, makes me realise I am crying. Tears blur my eyes.

I am alone. All alone. I feel so lost. I shove trembling hands deep in my jean's pockets and find what I should have found earlier. Used then. Prevented the dream from shuttering so soon. The nightmare from happening.

My cell. My hand closes around it. I turn it on. And I sob and sob and sob.

#2

The Barbican, London, UK.

It was Angeline Jollie who said "When the hopelessness is hurting you, it's the fixtures and fittings that finish you off." I wake up and feel I know what she meant when she said it. It's not my bed and it's not my T-shirt and my chest is hurting and my eyes are sore from too much crying.

I have nothing with me. No make up. No clothes. Just a set of keys I will no longer use after today and a wallet and a phone and suddenly no place to stay.

"Morning sweetie," the breezy voice snaps me to the present and I take in Mitch, short for Michelle, and the closest a girl can have to a best friend. Mitch is cool and tough and together. She likes girls and is not coy about it and works as a sculptress with some major London galleries vying for her pieces.

I am in Mitch's guest room and it's morning and it's London and it's raining. I usually love the rain even if it makes me sad. It feels good to feel it against you and hear it knocking against a window pane. With Ray I used to stay up and listen to it for hours sometimes and press myself against him and the thought now crashes me and without warning my eyes flood with tears that roll down my cheeks.

"Oh, sweetie,"

Mitch is at my side and a cup of black coffee has magically appeared and I feel that suddenly I love her and she just puts her arms around me and gives me someone to hold today and I smell the Chanel she wears and can't stop crying.

"He's not worth it, you know. No man is," she says and holds me.

I agree. But the tears are real. You think because you are a model and men are dying to get you into bed you have nothing to fear. The man who is with you loves you because you love him. I feel shattered. Betrayed. I can't help wondering how long it has been going on.

I see my phone and the light is blinking to let me know I have voice mail and I just can't handle it today. If I hear Ray's voice I'll die.

"You need a hot shower, then some shopping," Mitch smiles as she says that. "You have nothing to wear and until you go and pick up your stuff mine is a little big for you." Mitch is a size bigger at least and her taste in clothes has always been more severe than fun.

I watch her walk away and taste the coffee she left. It feels good. The bitterness makes my taste buds come to life. There is no milk and no sugar and the underlying taste of coffee beans carefully grounded and then filtered leaves me feeling at least as if I should make the effort, get out of bed and face the day.

Model

Alisa Miller

Mitch is a friend I have known for years. I was the one who introduced her to martial arts when I was using kick boxing for fitness and she became addicted to it. I have been shopping with her and have gone on blind dates with her when I would meet some guy and she would meet some girl and we'd probably made the least likely looking foursome in London. I have given her my bed to crash on when she was too wasted from drinking and partying and rejections she could not handle and I was there when she made her first large Gallery show in Scotland.

She never liked Ray and he did not like her and now I can only think I am glad he will not have her number. Here he cannot find me and this gives me time to decide and time to think.

Coffee. Shower. Hope.

Two of these three are relatively easy to come by and Mitch's bathroom provides everything I need except hope. The water is steaming hot and I stay under it, the shower in full blast and I do my favourite trick when I am unhappy or tired or feeling small: I stand absolutely still and slowly increase the hot water tap until, by degrees, it is on full, about as hot as I can handle it. I then reduce the cold water tap, acclimatising slowly, getting used to the heat. Feeling the power of the water striking me begin to heat up my body, its warmth seeping in deep inside me until I can swear I am sweating under the shower.

Alisa Miller

I read somewhere once that goldfish can be boiled alive. All you have to do is put them in a pot of water and increase the temperature gently, bringing it up to the boil a degree at a time. They continue to swim happily right up to the moment they die. Today I feel this is what I want to do here, now, I want to boil Ray from my memory and my body. I want to forget myself and the creep on the plane. I want to forget the photo shoot and the photographer and the guy with the fan who was his assistant.

And the hot water works its magic. I feel like it can go right through me cleansing me from everything that is bothering me right now and suddenly I am like alone, pure, bright and tired, good and vulnerable. I know I am not describing this too well right now but how can I describe a state of being which I have no words for?

Mitch's hot shower works its magic. I turn off the tap and step out of the cubicle and the bathroom is enveloped in thick steam from the shower and I have to open a window to let air in. It's cold and wet and fresh after the rain and it makes me shiver uncontrollably so I wrap a thick white towel around me and begin to look for a hair dryer and something to use on my hair.

Mitch's bathroom is fully equipped. Make up and hair-brushes and even unused, still sealed toothbrushes. I smile. Mitch is notorious for her pick ups and all night sex sessions and I now feel like she is the only friend I can turn to in the world.

Model

Alisa Miller

Unlike most other girls on the circuit I know Mitch is not a model and not direct competition and I really do not care if she sees me a wreck.

When I brush the steam off the mirror the face looking back at me is red with puffy eyes from too much crying and bright red lips from having bitten them too much. The eyes however look stronger than I thought and indeed, the shower I took has made it possible to face the day and look in the mirror and both of these are now an achievement.

***

Mitch smiles and wipes the froth of cappuccino coffee cream from her upper lip. John Lewis in Sloane square has always been a favourite haunt of mine and today, of all days, their coffee and in-premises baked shortbread chunks bring a glow inside me like they are food offerings which have dropped all the way from heaven.

"What are you going to do?" Mitch asks with her trademark candour and it focuses my mind.

"Few choices," I say, "Need to get my staff from Ray's, find somewhere to live and get some more work." All in that order. Over the past year I have taken fewer assignments than I usually would because living with Ray made me feel secure and safe and I hated spending time away from him. Now my bank balance is not as healthy as it would have been. I know I will have to ring my agent and explain. Then look for somewhere to rent. It all requires energy and suddenly I feel drained.

Mitch must see it in my eyes. She reaches across and takes my hand. Squeezes. "Men are pigs," she says it loud and her eyes are twinkling with mischief.

"Oh Mitch," I blurt.

"It's cool. Finish your coffee, let's go get you some threads at least. Can't have you going round naked in my house, you're way too much competition for me to handle."

She makes me laugh and I feel glad to have her as a friend.

The next few hours are spent in the comfortable womb of the John Lewis store. I have shopped at Macey's on Fifth Avenue and I have spent big money on Rodeo Drive but when it comes to feeling cosseted and welcome, unhurried and yet attended to, privileged and yet respected in terms of privacy, John Lewis stores are unrivalled.

As a treat to the ego and the bruised spirit of a girl they are so effective that I am convinced they should come with an NHS prescription. It would probably avert hundreds of suicides and thousands of depressions and save the country a cartload of money spent on dealing with the aftermath of these events.

So I shop, and walk and talk and smile and try on jeans and a mean leather jacket and UGG Boots and Ts and Cardys and we need to go to different departments in the store for each item and travel up and down its floors and the excitement and pleasure of it all makes me forget Ray and the pain and the fact that I am suddenly alone and that he has been a betraying bastard all along.

When we finish my phone rings and it's Ray and it's the first time he's tried to call since I ran out of the flat we had shared together.

I must have relaxed a little for I pick up. "Ali, I am sorry."

"Fuck you!" I cut him off and I hiss because John Lewis is crowded and this is not quite the image they want to project as far as the way their customers' behaviour is concerned.

"Ali, listen,"

"No you listen you son of a bitch. I'm gonna come round tonight and pick up my stuff."

"Ali, can't we talk about this? It doesn't have to be this way." I can't quite read his voice and it angers me.

"Yes that's the way it has to be. No one made you sleep with Cherisse you bastard. What you missed me too much and couldn't jerk off?" I have gotten angrier and my words are picked up and a couple of shoppers stop looking through the rows of dresses and look up. I catch a shop assistant out of the corner of my eye smirk a little and I flick my hair back. Fuck them too!

"Ali, please." He is at work so he can't say too much. Ray works in a bank. Barclays, on investments and acquisitions.

Alisa Miller

Acquisitions. Suits him.

"Tonight. I will get my stuff." I hang up.

That's it. It's done.

Of all the times I had broken up. The tears, the recriminations. The number of times I had men trying to ask me why. Why was I ending this affair? Why could I not stay with them? Why? Why? Why? And each time I had an excuse ready. Something which made them feel better. I had never felt ready to commit and men, well they are men. The moment they got too possessive I felt the urge to run. And now this. Ray was the first I had let my guard down with. I had loved playing house with him. Having dinner parties. Going to films. The past year had made me soft.

I dry swallow because it is hard. I had actually loved the bastard. I had given him my heart. I feel Mitch's hand on my shoulder and she gives me a friendly squeeze. "You ok?"

"Yeah," I nod. Time to pay for what I bought and head back home.

Home. Strange notion but I had never had a home.

I have been modelling since I was sixteen. Ads on TV. Magazine work, then swimsuits and lingerie. I like to run, swim. I do boxing. It keeps me fit and it shows. I get first refusal on work few other girls can get.

I have, since seventeen when I left home, been living from a suitcase and a bank account. I pay my own way, earn my own keep and those

Model

Alisa Miller

men who think I will be swayed by a fat wallet or a flashy car have always found out that I cannot be bought.

So now. Alone.

I am used to that. "Yeah, lets' go. I need to go and pickup my stuff," I say to Mitch and she follows me, her eyes checking out a John Lewis girl with long blonde hair and the figure of a waif.

The drive home is smoother than usual. Traffic is lighter than expected because it's just before five. In just a few minutes the roads will clog and London will live up to its name as the gridlock capital of Europe. Mitch drives carefully knowing how I hate dangerous driving and cars.

"Do you want to stay with me for a while?" she asks.

I look at her thinking about that. Last thing I want is pity today but Mitch's eyes are devoid of that.

"Just until you find a place," she says, "put your stuff in my office. The guest bedroom is free and I can use some company while I am finishing my next vase."

She's persuasive and I nod and she smiles and the arrangement gives me the strength to think of calling my agent. "I get the food bill," I say and she winks. My fingers find the speed-dial and I next call Neil.

Neil is forty and ageing badly but he is one of the best agents a model can have. He fights my corner in each job, making sure that I have everything I need and I am being taken care of.

Neil never travels. I doubt he's ever left Britain but I can also swear that his phone is glued to his ear.

He picks up on the first ring. "Ali! How was New York?" he asks, "Those creeps want you back."

He makes me smile. "How do you know they're creeps?"

"Oh you can tell a lot by the voice," he says and suddenly pauses. "You ok?"

"Yep, sure. Need some work fast."

"Money problems?"

"Man problems."

There is a momentary silence. "That dick never deserved you," he says at last, "He dumped you?"

"I'm dumping him."

"Screwing around?"

"He's a dick. You're right Neil."

Long pause, then: "You got a place to crash?"

His generosity makes my eyes brim. "I'm ok. I'm with Mitch."

"Give her my love and tell her if she ever gets tired of that old sow who manages her there is always a place in our books."

"I will Neil, thank you. Work?"

"I will get you some Ali, here or you want to fly again?"

"I need something fast."

"Ok, I understand. I will see what's best and call you tonight, ok?"

"Deal. Thanks Neil."

Model

Alisa Miller

"Stay cool kiddo. Shame I'm not younger."

It's been a running joke between us. I say thanks, hang up.

***

I look at the cardboard boxes containing my life in the middle of Ray's living room floor. He's not home yet and I have used the time to pack and now realise that maybe I need a break from Britain. Without Ray the weather and the pressure of people and the unsaid words in every sentence which need to be decoded for subtext can get to anyone after a while.

I am in the process of ringing Neil and telling him to book me for travel when I hear Ray at the door and freeze. This is now unfamiliar ground. I have seen the sheets in the bedroom still unmade and I wonder if he and Cherisse spent the night together after I left.

"Ali," he breathes.

I turn to look and he looks tired and for a moment I feel really glad and then I think what if he's tired because they stayed up all night having sex? And the thought makes the corners of my mouth twitch.

"I hate you!"

He doesn't answer immediately but his eyes are on the boxes and then he says: "Can't we talk about this Ali. I know I made a mistake,"

He sounds reasonable and smooth and confident under the strain and I remember that he's been trained to close deals worth millions of pounds and his negotiating skills are now being put to use to smooth over his love life.

I try to match his style: "Sorry, you made an irreparable mistake. You had a choice and you chose wrong."

"Ali, I know. I'm not asking for forgiveness, just a second chance."

"How long you've been sleeping with her Ray?"

"It only happened twice," he says and it's a stab at my heart.

"You bastard!" I hiss and have to clench my fists not to cry.

"Ali, it meant nothing."

That classic line. It means nothing. Why do men come out with it so glibly? Is it something that's drummed into them, the sort of catechism they learn at school? 'Repeat after me 1,000 times: sleeping with someone other than your partner means nothing.' I shall never know. To me it always means something. I don't sleep around when I am with someone. I could. I don't. Staying faithful means something. Sleeping around means something.

"Our life to you meant nothing," my words make him flinch and I find it suddenly satisfying.

I bend and pick up the first of the cardboard boxes and he steps in front of me barring the way out. "Ali, don't do this. We have a good thing going." It's the wrong thing to say just then.

"Yeah, you like it when I am here and, obligingly enough I have many hot friends and travel a lot."

"No, I-"

"Get out of my way."

"Why can't we just talk, get it out of our systems?"

"What like you got your dick out you mean?"

"Crude talk does not become you Ali,"

"Yeah, I forgot. It upsets you unless I am doing it to turn you on you prick!" and he hits me.

It's like a flash. My cheek hurts, then it's on fire. I am too shocked to speak for a split second and then the fury swells up inside me.

"You bastard!"

"Ali, I am sorry, I did not mean to-"

"Like hell you didn't," I drop the cardboard box I am carrying and kick him on the shin and he cries out and hobbles out of reach. I know he suddenly remembers that I do kick boxing every week when I am at home and I train every week and maybe, his height and weight are not that much of an advantage, though, in truth, they are.

I have no desire to get into a sparring match. I am shocked he hit me and 'didn't mean it' like he never meant to sleep with Cherisse and I just need to get out of there. Fast.

"Ali-"

Alisa Miller

My hiss cuts him off and he takes a step back. "Lay a hand on me you bastard, one hand again and I will cut your balls off," and I am angry and he can see it and my cheek is stinging and my eyes watering and I hate him and want him to die.

I get to the door and yank it open and for the second time in 48 hours I am running out of the apartment where I thought Ray and I had been so happy.

This time I stop downstairs and look at the doorman whose name I can't even remember. "Give this to Ray Stewart," I say and give him my key, "I will send for my stuff." He looks perplexed a little but is too professional to comment. He nods quickly and takes the key.

I am already heading for the nearby tube station and the taxi rank that's outside it. I feel that maybe things are better off this way. It's not the first time I am alone. I just need a little time to get through the details, pick myself up, salve my wounds and learn to survive again.

#3

The Barbican, London, UK.

In the modern world, if you're a model, you need a few things to survive: money, phone and a good agent. I needed the last two to make the first. It's all about connectivity and the ability to network. Neil was the best when it came to networking. Without leaving his office he was able, on any given day, to open doors and call favours across the Atlantic as well as London, Paris and Sydney.

Neil's girls got jobs fast. First refusal on major contracts and top pay for each job. But it did also mean that we were available at the drop of a hat, packed and ready to go where the job required us and we worked hard at not being difficult. In an industry were being difficult was always considered as part of your career move, we got first refusal because people liked working with us.

Ray's slap across my face had shattered a dream that now, in retrospect, appeared more fragile than an eggshell. How could I have been so stupid as to think that all I had to do was give complete, total unconditional love to someone and he would be the man for me?

I was smarting from the pain of my stupidity more than from any blow and I needed, really needed to feel needed again, badly.

Arranging to have my stuff picked up from Ray's took a few calls and a firm I felt I could trust to do the job. And I stand now at the window listening to my thoughts and waiting for Mitch to get back from the Gallery and thinking about what I should do next.

Idle hands do a devil's work and my phone rings just as I am thinking that maybe I should think about doing some cooking.

"Ali," I say.

"Ali it's Josh," the voice is jovial and I perk up a little. Josh is a party man in the sense that around him there is always some party going on or about to happen. He seems to have been thirty forever and no one quite knows what he does for a job.

"Joshie, where are you right now?"

"I'm at Craven Hill, opposite Paddington. You remember the place?"

I do. Josh has several apartments and I am probably one of the few who has been in every one of them.

"There's a party about to break out Ali," he speaks slowly, drawling out his words in a poor imitation of an American western twang. Josh is always playing around with enunciation and diction, impersonating characters and pretending to be someone else in his head.

Mitch thinks he is some kind of twisted freak, a serial killer in the making waiting for the right moment to come out. I think he is the only man who has not hit on me after knowing me for more than an hour and I just like his sense of humour.

"Are you for real Joshie?"

"Ali I swear. You're top of my list, I have like 100 calls to make still."

I giggle. He laughs.

"Be there in 50 minutes,"

"But Ali you're not that far-"

"I am Joshie. I'm at Mitch's. Ray and I do not exist any more." It's the first time I have said this openly to anybody since I caught Ray plundering Cherisse's honeypot and it feels cathartic to let it out.

He pauses, uncertain. "Oh,"

"It's cool,"

"For real?"

"For real Joshie."

"Cool!" and I giggle at that again. "Is Mitch coming with you?" he asks.

"No she's not home yet. Do you want me to leave her a note?" Mitch and Josh are not really that fond of each other.

"Naaaah, don't bother her. She's probably elbows deep in some vase. Come fast then Ali."

"50 minutes,"

He hangs up.

I stand for a split second considering what I have just done. A party is a party however and Josh does not lie. He does invite some of the most interesting people. Suddenly I do not feel so low any more. The chance to mingle with people and

Alisa Miller

listen to them talk, interact, feels me with a sense of excitement and I rush off to get dressed.

With my stuff still at Ray's or, more probably, on the way here, I have little to wear beyond what I bought at John Lewis' but one of the things I did buy was a little black dress without which a girl's wardrobe amounts to nothing, no matter how well it may be stocked. I have high-heels to match and I forego the clutchbag which is at Ray's at the moment.

I pause for a moment to toy with my hair in Mitch's large bedroom mirror and then I am kicking off my jeans and pulling the T over my head on my way to the bathroom.

I take my time with the shower letting it cleanse me psychologically as well as physically for the second time in as many days. When I step out I have already matched my outfit and I have a brand new black lace thong that'll match the dress.

Models always wear thongs, no matter what they throw on, on top. They are easy to put on, easy to take off. They do not show through any clothes, there is no visible panty line, they are easy to handwash when you are travelling and dry in what seems to be like minutes plus you can carry a month's supply in a padded A4 size envelope. As items of clothing go they are a must and on the sex-appeal front they are off the scale, rating higher than any bareback you care to mention. It's one of the reasons Jessica Simpson (who's been caught stepping in and out of cars wearing short little numbers) still has a lot of sex appeal whereas Britney Spears whose beaver has made front page news is really regarded to be way past it. Had Britney been a model as opposed to a pop diva she'd have known that the no-panties look is hot only with street walkers and girls who can't afford good quality thongs, to wear.

***

Joshie's party rocks the way he said it would.

I am now by the punch filling my glass and feeling happy.

I am towering on six inch heels and silver shoes, my flimsy black dress clinging to me in a way that makes me feel naked. I have matched it with a bracelet and tonight I am really missing the security of having a clutchbag, I ignore it and carefully fill my glass with punch.

"Can I help?" it's a new voice, suave and confident. I turn to look. He's about 35, wearing the polo neck signature of the fashion director. I wonder who for.

"Hi," I smile. He takes it as a yes and takes the ladle from me, expertly stirs the punch and fills both our glasses.

"Josh sure knows how to throw a party," he motions casually around the room.

Josh's apartment is filled with people. There are people out in the covered terrace and people in the living room and the kitchen. The music in the background, all pervasive and tasteful forms a constant backdrop plus people are always coming and going. Every time I look up from my drink I can swear the demographics in the room have changed again.

When I got there, there were more banker types. A couple wanted my number. Once invited me to his yacht. Still fresh from Ray I am giving bankers a wide birth for now.

A little later there was the guru crowd. Some Yoga club owner and her instructors, a couple of photographers and a fitness video director. He wanted me to be in one of them.

Now it was more mixed with indiscernibles.

"Bet you're in fashion," the guy says and then as an afterthought: "James,"

"Ali," I say.

"The heels," he explains as if I've asked him, "They are incredible."

"I model," I offer.

"The 'totally naked' lingerie? I saw it." There is a slight amused twinkle in his eye and I inwardly sigh. The Totally Naked lingerie campaign was on all the billboard ads in London, they are doing the same thing now in New York. It's the kind of fame a girl can do without. Guys think that because you earn your living being photographed with hardly any clothes on you are a natural for saying 'yes' to any offer of sex you receive.

"Which set?" I ask.

"Excuse me?"

"Which set did you see, the white one or the black one?" – It had been the Ad Director's idea. Photograph me in one of each. The Angel and the Demon. That way they would alternate between weeks.

"The black one," he smiles.

The black lingerie was more revealing. The material finer. I wax everywhere, religiously, once every ten days. Better than shaving, no razor burn to contend with and no unsightly body hair. The sheer fine silk of the black set showed that I waxed, very clearly.

"Well, at least I don't have to introduce myself formerly then," I say.

"It must be hard getting all this attention all the time. You must think every man's a total jerk."

"No, not every man..."

"But most, I get it."

I smile because what can I say to that and I sip from my glass.

"You haven't asked what I do."

"What do you do?"

"I'm a talent scout," he says.

It's the oldest line in the book and I think well, he is going to be easy to brush-off but he has seen it and is quick to move in.

"It's not a line. Here." He gives me his card.

Ron C. Charles IV
Talent Development Director
Joyce Johnson Entertainment Inc.

There is an email and a phone number. The email indeed goes through the JJ website. The guy appears legit.

"Talent Development Director?" I quiz and he smiles. I find his smile open, honest. A lot of people smile in London. It is the ubiquitous gesture of business. People smile when they want something from you. They smile when they want to offer you something. They smile before they close a deal. They smile before your contract is cancelled. They smile after taking you to bed and they smile when they say they do not want to see you again.

London people smile for many different reasons. I smile back.

"You have such great eyes," he says it in a straightforward way.

"What does a Talent Development Director at JJ?" I ask.

"I ask myself that every morning," he says and I giggle. It is funny. "But seriously, I rubber stamp detailed suggestions on building celebrity profiles and entertainment hostesses."

"Like the MTV presentations?" I ask.

"Yep, the very same. We placed Nataly there."

Model

Alisa Miller

"And you just rubber-stamp it all?"

He smiles again. I find his smile endearing. Surreptitiously check for a ring, see none but that means nothing in these circles. I've had my share of marriage surprises the morning after the night before. My gay radar is finely tuned and Ron is definitely not gay. At the moment he ticks all the right boxes apart from the fact that Ron sounds much like Ray but three letter names are all the rage at the moment and even those who have not got one are shortening them to fit in so I can't really hold it against him.

"Do you want to get out of here?" he asks. "I know a club."

"Discreet?"

"You're married?" he asks and smiles to show he knows the answer to that already. "It's relatively quiet," he says, "you can talk as well as dance."

"Ok," and I have myself a date for the night.

***

Ron's apartment across the Thames is probably worth more than entire city blocks cost in most towns. The view is magnificent. The lights of the river make everything look like it should be a prop in a film. It has the glossy quality, the depth and feel which somehow real life does not easily convey.

Alisa Miller

I feel him running his tongue down my spine and involuntarily shiver. He has been a man of his word. The club we went to was quiet enough to talk and the music good enough to dance to. And he surprisingly proved himself to be competent enough in both departments.

We drunk and danced and drunk some more. When you are a model you have to remind yourself to eat. Dance and booze are plentiful and easy to find. Unless you get some alone time you do not often get the opportunity to have a proper meal. I had had a few of the snacks and complicated looking appetisers at Josh's party but it was way past the witching hour and no model worth her salt ever lets food pass her lips after 10.00pm at night.

When we came out of the night club it was three in the morning and the prospect of catching a lone ride to Mitch's suddenly seemed very unappealing.

So here I am and Ron's hands are travelling over the contours of my body. He cups and squeezes my buttocks and he gets really excited because his body is then pressed against mine from behind and I can feel him rock hard. It always fascinates me to see how men react to my body. I work hard to stay trim and fit because of my profession. I see my body everyday, I work on it in one way or another and after a while I tend to take it for granted.

Model

Alisa Miller

Ron is so excited his breathing is laboured and his hands are trembling.

"You are so beautiful," he says and then buries his face in the small of my back. His hands squeezing wherever they travel.

Men are funny creatures. They work hard to take you to bed and then, when it happens, they get so excited they forget to stay in charge. It's like they revert to some atavistic past where they are little boys needing to be told what to do. I can see that unless I make the first move Ron is quite capable of touching me and squeezing me and licking me until morning.

I slowly feel around and find him and he gasps. I arch my back and pull him towards me, guiding him. He has had the courtesy to use protection and I can feel the pulse in his penis in my hand, through the thin latex of the condom.

When he finally enters me he gasps like it's his first time and his body convulses and his hips grind suddenly, hard, against me. He lasts about two minutes before he explodes inside me and goes limp against me.

I slowly pull away to go and use the bathroom.

In the bedroom bathroom mirror I look tired. My eyes drawn more than usual. "You need to get some sleep," I say to the naked reflection looking back at me. I momentarily see me as men see me. Breasts high and very firm (and I know this is genetics). Shoulders, slightly athletic from the hours of heavy bag work and gym training.

Alisa Miller

Arms firm and my body tapering down to a narrow waist. Then the slight curve of my hips.

I reflect momentarily on just how lucky I am in terms of my shape. Women are born to have wide hips. If your skeletal structure is like that there is nothing you can do about it. Models have slim hips. I wonder if mother nature is selecting against child birth and for beauty.

It's a funny thought to have after sex so late at night.

I use Ron's shower and towel myself dry feeling the fresh energy the shower gives you seep into me. When I get back into the bedroom Ron is deeply asleep, on his back, snoring lightly and I let myself into the bed. It's big enough for neither of us to have to snuggle against the other and I then slowly unplug, let my body go limp and feel as if my very soul is oozing out of me. Vanishing, dying.

I sleep naked and the thought occurs to me that it might make for a sense of awkwardness first thing in the morning. After all, I have just met the guy. The thought evaporates as I drift into the warm, fuzzy arms of sleep.

#4

Berkley Square, Mayfair, London.

The morning after the night before is always a little funny. You look at the guy and you're not sure what to say. Some of them think you will make a scene. Others are concerned with how to best get you out the door fast. And there are those who want to make sure they see you again but want to also make sure you understand that it does not constitute a proposal for marriage.

Ron was of the latter category. He was wearing a T-Shirt that was oversized and hid his boxer shorts. On a guy it always looks funny no matter how expensive it is. He hovered over the bedroom doorway suddenly shy and unsure. I've noticed this about men. The more sure and cocky they are in their work life the more insecurities they harbour when their clothes come off.

I get up and let the sheets slide off me and I see the gasp on his face which he struggles to control as he sees my body in daylight. I swing right past him, lingering long enough to plant a kiss on his cheek.

'Morning,' I whisper. He dry swallows, tries to act cool but he is totally unsure. I know he watches me, his eyes glued, all the way to the bathroom where I shut the door.

When you are a girl the whole world's a stage.

I run the shower boiling hot and when I finally get back out he is dressed in dark suit and polo neck, now in control and trying to act superior.

"Ali, that was-"

I let the towel drop and he stops his eyes in danger of popping out of his head. I pretend I do not notice and casually spend time getting dressed. Last night's clothes are all over the floor on one side of the bed and I make sure I take my time to put them on. The thong is different and I smile at the thought of underwear which is small enough to fit seamlessly in a pocket and get swapped the next day has to be simply a gift from above.

When I finish I know that if I were to ask Ron to marry me there and then he would agree and sign my prenup before he even considers calling his lawyers. On the event I know I need to get to Mitch's and get my head together so I just ask him for a lift.

"Will I see you tonight?" he asks in the car. Ron drives a black Mercedes SLK, two seats and the cream leather interior screams expensive.

"I need to get some work," I smile, "I recently lost my house so now I need to make sure I can afford to buy one myself."

"Oh?"

"Boyfriend problems,"

"Oh."

"History,"

"Ok."

Model

Alisa Miller

I know he is now trying hard to come up with what to say next so I take pity and save him the trouble. "I will call you depending on the kind of day I have, deal?"

"Deal," he looks relieved and a little confused.

***

It's easy to be critical of the fact that I so easily made the transition from Ray to Ron. Just one letter, right? It's a joke. When things get tough I always find it that I can joke about myself. I don't know why but it has kept me sane so it's a defence mechanism I have learnt to hone, but I digress. I am about to explain how I went from Ray to Ron, from angry and broken to sleeping with a guy I had just met.

It makes me smile when I think that every time I try to explain something like this to anyone they come out with some moral judgement like there is a natural law or some religious edict about doing it. The Bible is full of tales of unbridled sex which seems to cross all lines of propriety and to put sleeping with some one on the same level as unlawfully killing somebody reeks of the kind of narrow-minded, ignorance and femiphobia that fuelled the Spanish Inquisition witch-hunts.

No one likes being alone. And loneliness has a way of creeping in under you skin and undermining everything you are. The higher you fly the lonelier you get. I have been on photo shoots where the champagne was flowing and the music was great and the atmosphere was top of the world and the moment the camera lights went out and the photographers left you are on your own putting on jeans and Ts and feeling like you have been abandoned by the world.

Physical connections are easier to forge than spiritual ones. They are a substitute though which is easier to come by. I know what people think. The moment they start to think about it religion and morality and judgment all go hand in hand and if you pause and think about it logically this holds about as much water as a bucket without a bottom.

It may be immoral to steal and it is certainly immoral to kill. Lying and cheating and being double-faced have a place in some ill-defined, ever-moving, gray area of our moral compass. Sleeping with someone certainly has nothing to do with morality. Sex is a means of self-expression, a cry for help, a call for attention, a need for tenderness and, even, a means of self-destruction. Morality has nothing to do with any of this and those who seek to hide behind such judgments have unresolved issues of their own which they are unable to face. As a result they externalise it, project their own sense of inner guilt and inadequacy upon others and then dress it up for public consumption so they can recruit those around them.

It always sounds like a witch-hunt because it is.

I left home at sixteen because I could not stand hypocrisy and my whole life I have tried to be open and honest, dealing with others the way many are unable to deal with me. Modelling is a tough career. You have to have the acting skills of a Hollywood star, the toughness of a quarterback, the resilience of a boxer and the endurance of a marathon runner. Plus you need to be size zero, despite what fashion editors say, and know how to walk on three-inch high heels without sprawling on the catwalk.

Still think it's easy being a model? The fame that gets you there is also the fame which can destroy you. After a while the loneliness and the betrayals, the bitchiness and the catfights, the constant come-ons, judgements and rejections, they all take their toll.

I have friends I started with who now live in rehab permanently. I have friends I started with who got chewed up and spat out by the lifestyle and the industry. The way I see it there are two things you can do: shut up and survive or get out.

Ron had broken my heart. I had began to go soft, was thinking of getting out. If I stopped and thought and felt the loneliness, the depth of his betrayal, the wasted time, I would fall apart in a million little pieces. Frey had it so right, even if it was fictional. I was not going to fall apart and I was not going to get out unless it was on my own terms. That's why I made a call to Dr Aaronson.

***

"Ali you need a little time to think about the future you," Dr Aaronson's voice oozes authority, integrity and trust and I lap it up like I have always done.

James Aaronson is barely 50. Grizzled, lean, dressed in perpetual black sweaters. He reminds me of model shoot designers now that I have modelled long enough to know who they are and what they do and they normally look like.

I am sure James Aaronson invented the look long before they did like he pioneered a whole lot of other things in the dozen studies he has carried out and the hundreds of papers he has published and the dozens of books he has written. He was my mentor in my final year at Uni and he helped me through the difficult task of the inward journey which every psyche student has to undertake. He is therefore my cornerstone. The person I turn to for guidance when I am lost within myself.

"There is not a lot of time for anything these days," I hear myself say and he smiles as he sees me echo the issue that's troubling me and the realization dawns.

"See now?"

I really do not know how he does it. We have been talking here for two hours, going through my discovery of Ray with our neighbour, my feelings of loss and dread, my anxiety and inability to focus, my finding Ron and going to bed with him. James Aaronson has been listening, nodding, prodding, questioning, guiding, holding himself up as a mirror for me to see my own actions in.

I see now. I see exactly what I need to see and seeing him has been exactly what I needed.

"You know you are breathtakingly beautiful," he says it as a statement and coming from him it is a judgment that makes me smile.

#5

XY Gym, South Kensigton, London.

It hurts. The pain helps me stay anchored in the here and now. This is about as real as it gets. When I want to be alone I do what I have always done: I run. I am more suited to short distances. Speed and power but that's for fun. What I do to keep fit. To think I need space and I need time and I find both when I do long distances and uphill.

The gym is practically empty at this time of the morning and I have been there many times before. The owner is a close friend of mine and today I do not even need to ask to be left alone. He knows my moods and he knows how I feel and he knows that what I want is to lose myself in the effort.

The treadmill is new. Its motor powerful. The 12km/hr speed close to true. The incline is 2.5% which means I climb 2.5 metres for every 100 I run. In a kilometre that's 250 and by the time I am done I will have climbed 1,250 metres.

That's why there is pain.

Lungs are labouring but not yet burning. That'll come later. For now there is the heavy flow of breath in and out as I pump my arms to maintain the pace and keep up with the incline by bringing my knees up as I run. I have always found that the physical effort involved helps my mind stay focused and get clear.

Model

Alisa Miller

I pump my arms and run and run and slowly the pain, though it increases, becomes harder to register. What is left then is me: pure thought. Mind free of the body. Thinking and through thinking being. Most people think models are all looks. We spend all day doing our hair and fretting over our makeup. Not true. We sense the possibilities opened by our looks. We see the chances which are coming our way and want to simply make the most of it. Now.

Time is always against us and we know it.

There is a thing about sensing possibilities and experiencing potential. You never know exactly what you need to do and in what order. This is the pressure of our lifestyle. What drives so many of us to drink, drugs and...sex.

It is sometimes easier to self-destruct than self-construct.

I know that in myself which is why I am now experiencing pain. Physical pain helps keep me real. It helps anchor me in the present. It fixes my body in time and thus frees my mind so that I can think.

And think I do.

I've spent the last five years going from one exotic photoshoot to another, living out of a suitcase. I need to change this now before it begins to consume me. As my body runs my mind travels. I see that there are choices I have and they are all as pressing as they are clear. I could, I suppose, press my modelling success home but while I dominate in the lingerie and swimsuit scene going further up the chain, opening shows worth hundreds of thousands of dollars is something which will require more than looks.

In modelling you don't just sell your looks. There are a thousand girls as pretty as you, as pouty as you and as willing to work hard as you, all waiting to be discovered. If you are making headway and you are a model you know that your success lies in your ability to do two things: 1. Stay in character. The moment the clothes, the lingerie or the swimsuit go on you become a girl who is coming from somewhere and going somewhere, someone with a complex story and a past and a future all written in her poise and face and it is this which creates the allure (or at least part of it). 2. Be a character. We live in the age of the product. Models are products and the ones who open shows and command huge contracts are the ones who put in time and effort into creating a brand out of their name and their life.

Designers and cosmetic companies do not want just a pretty face. They can use their in-house staff for that, if that's all they need. No. What they need, above all else, is a brand. A personality. A product. Models who understand the requirements usually go far.

As a model who wants to climb to the top of her profession you know that everything you do, think, dream and sleep has to do with your work and how to turn your name, life, looks and lifestyle into a brand that helps sell clothes and make cosmetics look sexy.

It is a tough way of living. One which requires perhaps more sacrifices than I am willing to make.

I spent years studying psychology, graduating just a few months back, training as a relationship counsellor so that I would not be just a piece of performance merchandising.

The treadmill machine beeps to mark the reaching of the 5km mark and I slap the emergency stop button with the flat of my hand to make it slow down and stop. The treadmill does not stop immediately. It takes a few seconds and I realize that it takes a huge effort to slow down with it at the same rate. My limbs suddenly feel heavy. My lungs are aching, feeling bruised.

I stop and stare at the blinking red numerals showing the distance I have just run and the heaviness of my body, the sudden fatigue that sips in, the incremental pain which floats back to my awareness. Altogether, they form a matrix against which I can now visualise myself and feel that what I have done, what I have achieved is real and my head is clear.

Through the pain and the gasping for breath, with sweat running down my forehead and into my eyes I realise that I know what I need to do. I know what the only option left for me is. I know where I am going, at last.

When I run I wear as little as I can safely get away with. In this case a special running top

Alisa Miller

with in-built support by Nike in hot pink and a skimpy pair of black towelling shorts made by Wicked Weasel. It tends to draw attention but that is part of being a model anyway and I refuse to blend just because someone may think that it's too daring an outfit for a gym. I take the view that I pay my membership fee just like everyone else so if they do not like it they can lump it.

I finally step off the treadmill, towel round my neck and thankful for the insight I have suddenly gained. My priorities after running are always immediate: 15 minutes of sauna and then a long, luxuriant shower with a progressively colder and colder temperature. By the time I come out of the shower my skin is glowing, my body reacting to the cold has upped its circulation and despite the fatigue I feel the most alive I have felt all week.

***

We all feel the need for validation. There is the pressure of work which keeps us all reacting. The simple fact that we need to live, pay the rent, buy food, have money for clothes. These things tend to focus the mind and even a model has bills to pay.

Then there is what we do which tends to define, partly what we are. There is a risk here which is clearly occupational. Models tend to think that the job is them. The job is simple: project, act,

Model

Alisa Miller

become. We look at a set of clothes, an outfit, an accessory and we project a role into the person wearing that.

We can become, in an instant, hostess, wife, call girl, bad girl, secretary. Whatever the role requires in order to make the clothes sell. Put me in transparent lingerie and I think mistress, sex kitten, sex-slave. I project an appeal which I can see draws a response. Give me PJs with a flower pattern and I think innocence, girl-child. I become that and people respond.

It's fun.

It's also a mind-fuck. Unlike actors who have the luxury of time to 'get into the part' and then have a wind-down period to get out of it a model has seconds to think, research, assimilate and project. We are chameleons who happen to look good. Taken us out of our job we are no more beautiful than the girl next door.

It's one reason why models can make such good actresses. René Rousseau, Evangeline Lilly, Famke Janssen and Cameron Diaz to mention but a few. We learn to do exactly what's needed for the role. It's also one reason some of us self-destruct so easily. When it's hard to switch off the only way you have of knowing that you are real is when you feel the pain of hurting yourself.

Kate Moss does drugs and cigs and men and she's the cheerleader for the rest of us. We are locked into a cycle where unless we have some purpose we are cast adrift into the night, still acting, still being not us, even when we are with other people.

Do this often enough and you find that without the cigs, the men and the drugs you really do not know who you are.

The thoughts that go through my head as I negotiate through the tortuous London traffic serve to distract me from the ache of my body. Muscles are feeling bruised, pushed to the limit and complaining. I know that for me the drug of choice has been a mix of men and training. I don't smoke and I don't do drugs. I stopped doing men when I met Ray and thought, like an idiot, that he was 'the one', and whenever I feel low or lost or tired or sick of the world or simply need to find the real me again because too many jobs and too many parties and too many late nights have taken their toll, I train. Hard. Real hard.

Pain helps keep you real. Anchored to the world.

That's how it works for me.

As I am driving and the exhaustion seeps in and through me and I have to blink fatigue away I begin to feel the real me seeping back into every fibre of me and I begin to feel again just how I belong to the world.

I have been modelling since I was seventeen. My first shoot was swimwear for teens and it was the year I lost my virginity.

Some memories stay with you longer than others.

Model

Alisa Miller

Coconut Grove in Miami is the place where the rich and famous hang out. Two floors above where I was staying Jay-Lo maintained an apartment and the one I was living in came with a Porsche Boxster as part of the set up. The photo shoot was for the latest catalogue by Teen Brides, an up-market Miami swimwear and lingerie outlet which catered to those who had more money than sense.

I was too young back then to wonder aloud if teen brides really went for this kind of thing or if Teen Brides was a clever marketing edge designed to gain valuable publicity through the promotion of a controversial brand name. At the time I was too intent on learning what it was that I had to do. I wanted to succeed.

The shoot was over two days and it featured expensive boat decks. One of Miami's most exclusive Marinas was our backdrop and prop. I was one of three other models and the amount of attention we were getting was heady.

Thinking back upon it as I am driving I want to say to myself that I was stupid. Back then I couldn't. You are young, impressionable, eager to please and eager to learn. You think that if you play fair everyone else will play fair with you and that is your game plan with the world.

The photographer was Miguel Fernando, one of Miami's most sought-after names. I guess now I would call him a Cuban sleezeball more interested in booze and young girls than art but back then I thought he was like Picasso with a camera. He had flair, style and a way that made you think you were the centred of his universe and in the whole wide world you were the only person who really mattered.

At seventeen this is power you can never hope to handle. Like too much speed in the bloodstream it makes you feel brave, beautiful, wanted. It makes you feel invulnerable and knowledgeable and, most stupid of all, it makes you feel wise.

Nadia, one of the other models was a former Russian athlete. She had a body which was lithe like a snake, with clean muscles which moved as she walked and her straight blonde hair went down to her waist. I remember thinking to myself how unfair it was that there were women shaped like that. She had a funny way of talking, drawing her words out and letting her Russian accent sex them up.

"You seem to be drawing more attention than the rest of us," she said to me with a twinkle in her eye. I did not really know what to reply so I just nodded. We were below decks in a yacht which in any other part of the world would house three families, getting changed in the owner's cabin. "Watch yourself with Miguel darling,"

She was casual about the way she looked naked and totally natural when up on deck. She was a year older than me but at eighteen she behaved much older. I already knew she had a reputation for gobbling up men and spitting them

Model

Alisa Miller

out and looking at her, back then, confident, beautiful and utterly poised, I felt that she was someone I could emulate. A role model to guide me as I tried to find my place in the world.

"He is cute," I said and smiled. Nadia was slipping into a one-piece which seemed designed to reveal more than it hid.

"Miguel? Yeah darling," she said answering her own question, "he is also a barracuda, eats up model girls for breakfast, lunch and dinner. Watch yourself,"

I watched her perfectly shaped ass disappear up the ladder leading to the deck and I wondered just how I should take her advice.

At seventeen I was no prude. But studying, modeling, travelling and the pressure to keep fit had left me with no steady relationship, no boyfriend and a condition which was more frequently encountered in Mills & Boon romantic novels than in modern life. I had yet to go all the way with someone and it was beginning to bug me.

There is a truism of our age which holds for many things: the virtues of the past are the vices of the present. For me, virginity was beginning to be a problem which I had to solve as fast as possible.

#6

The Barbican, London, UK.

Mitch is home and frowning in that special frown I know precedes a lecture. After running I feel cool. Muscles ache, each breath stretches bruised lungs and my blood is singing with endorphins. I smile and know that my eyes are ringed in black.

"Racoon look hot this year," confirms Mitch and I smile a wider smile. I know she cares and I do not want to hurt her feelings and yes, I am tired and when I get so my eyes have dark rings underneath like I have not slept for a week.

"Running kills Mitch," I exhale and let the words draw themselves out and her frown gets deeper.

"You won't get any work looking like a panda bear," she says and follows me as I go to the room I have taken over. She hovers in the doorway and watches me undress, look for clothes, dress. She may be cataloguing me with her eyes but she's a friend and I have felt worse eyes than hers on me before and I stay unconcerned.

"How do you do that?" she asks.

"Do what?"

"Zone out like that. It's like you edit me out of the picture and you are alone in the room with all your clothes around your feet."

"I'll pick them up,"

"That's not what I am asking,"

Model

Alisa Miller

I smile and stop and stare back at her and she goes red. That moment in time I so love Mitch. I love that she cares and craves in equal measures and I think then just how bloody complicated we all are. Products of a world which is more complicated than we can ever know and where the simple things cost money to enjoy.

"It's a trick you learn when you model,"

"Aaah, zoning out the creeps,"

I smile again.

"Bet they undress you with their eyes even before you get your kit off,"

"It's the job. They come with the territory,"

"Should be outlawed in lingerie photo shoots,"

Mitch knows about some of the stories I have told her and is right. The men who hang about are a little unsavoury and the parties afterwards descend into Roman orgies only with more money and less class. I bend to pick up the clothes I dropped and wince with the ache I feel in my lower back.

"You know I need the money and it's what I am good at,"

"Yep, you also have a brain Ali and you've done all that damned hard studying,"

Point well made Mitch. I do have a brain for what it's worth and for the last year I conveniently parked it in idle as I spent time with Ray and played at being a good housewife.

There is a buzz from my bedside table and we both look at the vibrating Blackberry.

"That evil contraption of yours,"

Mitch cannot do tech. Blackberrys give her headaches and all she can do is click to talk and click to hang up which is why she has a Nokia that does just that. Me, without my daily dose of tech I'd go mad. My Blackberry is my office and mobile helper all rolled into one, without it I would be totally lost.

I pick up and check the email that's arrived.

It's Ron and he is all smiles. The Blackberry respects the settings and I have programmed it to strip icons from messages. The full colon and close bracket punctuation that Ron has used to create a smiley face gets annoying after the first three lines.

TV CONTRACT ....THAMES TV..... ONE TIME GIG .... U IN?

I think about it. I suppose a contract ought to come in something a little more substantial than an email with smileys, then again I did sleep with him and he is now feeling a little sheepish. He needs to sound out the water before he pushes it for real.

I sigh inwardly to myself. Men! They never grow up.

I fire off a brief reply that says 'yeah, sure. Please tell me more.' Then check the next email in line and see my agent has not failed me. There is a photo shoot being organised in St Petersburg – three day run, quick in, quick out - $25,000 on the table. Agent Provocateur are the organiser. The way he describes it, it sounds like a clandestine operation against the state. The money's ok and I think that St Petersburg, this time of the year, is not going to be any worse than staying in London.

Agent Provocateur are expensive lingerie and I know from previous shoots that their gigs are always mega-dollar affairs which attract a lot of publicity. It's a good platform and I say yes. 'Arrange my visa' I ask and lock the Blackberry.

Memories come unbidden. Fatigue and excitement do weird things to a person's mind.

"This your first time on a boat this size?" Miguel's accent sounds sexy to my ears but his choice of words almost makes me giggle. Even at seventeen I analyzed syntax and speech patterns and men's preoccupation with size is something which really makes me laugh. The biggest car, the biggest boat, the longest cigars, the biggest dick. They are all obsessed with this comparison drive which makes me thing we are still on the playground and are holding plastic toy trucks. The kid with the biggest one always won on the impression stakes. He got to have the most friends.

Miguel sauntered into view, shirt half unbuttoned to the waist. He was slim, like a dancer but with nothing like the musculature and the hair on his chest was wispy. He held a bottle of champagne in one hand, two glasses in the other.

We were alone.

The photo shoot had ended two hours ago and the girls had left on the speedboat to get back to their hotels. "Want to stay for a few more shots darling?" Miguel had asked, "free ones, for your portfolio."

It was a lame attempt. From a professed pro I would have expected much better but he did not call the shots on this, I did, so I smiled sweetly and nodded like a dumb school girl would.

The atmosphere was fantastic. There was a crew of three on the boat which I found in turns both unnerving and exciting. I was a sole girl in the company of four men, at sea. I fantasized that anything could happen. They could, for all I knew, take turns taking me and then dump my body at sea.

A little simplistic. One of them was a chef. He cooked a marvellous meal of steamed shrimp, oysters and a light vinaigrette salad, served with a light champagne with a slightly fruity taste.

Not having eaten for almost twenty-four hours prior to the photo shoot I felt the first glass go straight to my head.

"A little more?" Miguel leaned solicitously towards me, his eyes gleaming and he re-filled my glass. Maybe it's not cool for a girl to plan how to lose her virginity so that she is no longer stigmatized by it but it has to happen sometime, right? And it is always best that it happens for the best of reasons, or rather for the right reasons as opposed to the wrong ones.

I downed my first glass, asked for a refill. Drunk more than half of it before the food arrived.

Model

Alisa Miller

By the time I was on my third I was finding Miguel's company stimulating and his conversation witty. He spent time telling me about his first wife. A model I'd never even heard of who was distantly related by marriage to the Kennedy clan.

"Bitch darling," he was saying, "can you believe it? Took me for all I had after all I did for her."

Looking at him leering I felt he actually deserved it. I started wondering vaguely what he would feel like and whether he would first ask me for oral sex. Now, while not yet having gone all the way at seventeen I had had my share of opportunities to experiment and I had taken them all willingly.

Hanging around models and their hanger ons, looking at what goes on and never missing a party I had had, I guess, about six boyfriends by then who had never pressed me enough for me to say 'yes' to the ultimate question but who had, nevertheless, availed themselves of my willingness to learn and try as much as possible.

Miguel, I imagined, by his demeanour would not be the kind who grabbed your hair and pulled your head down to his waist. He looked more of the fondling, fumbling type, hands and tongue everywhere.

Men have used alcohol as a failsafe aphrodisiac since time immemorial, and women have let them. I am not going to go into the right and wrong of this. We all need, sometimes, to feel we have lost control, that what will happen next is not entirely the result of a conscious decision on our part. It sounds a little pathetic, I know, but I have been around people long enough to know that we all struggle to avoid growing up. That's why we have alcohol... and drugs. They both do the same thing: they allow us to lose control in a way which absolves us of responsibility and justify, somehow, what we do then.

Drugs are a rather extreme way to achieve this. They last only a short time and leave some pretty undesirable side effects. Alcohol, being socially approved, comes with a kind of green light which you don't get with drugs. Plus it's easy to get hold of and the real intentions behind its use can be disguised.

Steamed mussels and shrimps go very nicely with champagne and by the time my third glass was over Miguel's company was beginning to look perfect. Alcohol had worked its effect on him too. He had lost some of the leering and his face had taken on a more earnest look as he detailed to me his plans and told me what he liked doing and what he'd like to do in the world of fashion photography.

He'd touch my hand as he spoke and his eyes had a sincerity which I found endearing. "Girls always think that you want them for their bodies," he said, "but I'll tell you a secret darling. There is more to it than just that. If all men want is a sexy body we could always hire a pro to come and screw our brains out you know," he paused to see the effect of his words, suddenly worried that he might have gone too far.

At seventeen the world is still new to you You lap up everything like a sponge because every experience, even a potentially bad one feels fresh and exciting and with something new to say. "Go on,"

"What we really want from a woman is the thing we cannot have. Not sex, but her. The person she is. We want to feel that deep connection, sense the innocence and passion she has, the ability to be deeper than us. And when we take her we feel that we lose part of ourselves, darling. I can't really explain it to you more. It's like we give some part of us which never comes back and in giving it we gain a little inner peace." He paused and looked at me again, his eyes, blinking, were suddenly like a child's. He felt much younger than me. More innocent.

"Was it like that with your ex?" I asked.

"Yes, more so. I really loved her. Caught her screwing my best friend."

I could have asked more then. The time for words had passed. Without talking I stood up, picked up his hand. Pulled him behind me as I headed for the boat's master bedroom.

There was a natural resistance to Miguel which I suddenly found really touching. "You want this, right?" I asked. I had to make sure.

"Darling..." his voice sounded choked. His throat tight.

Model

Alisa Miller

Much, much later, when I could reminisce about that night I often marvelled at the way the tables had been reversed and how something which would normally have been fairly traumatic and perhaps a little exploitational, had turned into a night where I had learned so much about men and, in the process, finally become a woman.

The boat's master cabin was phenomenal. Lights and glass everywhere. Mirrors to make it look bigger. Light   mahogany panelling and expensive carpeting. A plush bed dominating the room.

I made Miguel sit on the edge of it. Stood back and slowly peeled off my top. Dropped in on the floor. Slid my jeans off and stood back. I had not bothered with a bra and the thong I had on was minimal. I had recently modelled for Wicked Weasel. A swimsuit and underwear company working out of Byron Bay in Sydney, Australia. They had been so pleased with the results of the catalogue shoot that they had given me $1,000 worth of underwear. The entire collection of everything I had bought with their generous offer fit comfortably in my handbag. They did not believe in using a lot of fabric in their creations.

"Wow!" Miguel breathed out.

I smiled. Slowly turned on the spot, letting him see what he would get. His breath caught at the back of his throat. He fumbled with the buttons of his shirt.

Model

Alisa Miller

"Let me," I said. I leaned over him, the tips of my breasts beckoning, long blonde hair swimming towards him. He let me take control, his hands on my hips, caressing, going round me as I leaned forwards to cup my buttocks. Squeeze.

His shirt was off now and he was breathing hard, like he'd been running. He raised his head and his lips, eager to please, found my nipples.

"God," he whispered.

I undressed him.

His hands had already moved my thong down to my knees. I felt eager fingers seek to get inside of me. I gently restrained him. He looked up.

"Here," I said, I climbed on top of him, my underwear slipping off completely, pushed to the floor with the toes of one foot. I straddled him, felt his hot breath, looked in his eyes and then gasped as he opened his mouth and his long tongue reached out to taste me, his hands already cupping my breasts, squeezing and kneading, urgently stoking the passion in me.

He was sweet and gentle and eager and passionate. He gasped and sighed and gasped again and his breath came in laboured whizzes as I goaded him, licked, sucked, nibbled on him, encouraged him to taste and touch and explore everywhere.

Most men need some guidance. Very few are sure enough of themselves to really take control and those who do are rarely worth the effort.

Model

Alisa Miller

When I finally lay back and parted my legs, drew him with one hand inside, guiding him, Miguel was ready to explode. He entered me like a rocket, hardly able to contain himself. The moment he inserted in me drew a gasp from him as well as me.

He held me down, his grip on me steadying me as I felt the searing pain. Cried out with it. Felt the rawness inside me as he began to move.

I am more than certain that he had not realised I was a virgin. His rising and falling above me shook me like a rag doll. His hands squeezed and pinched and grabbed and fondled and his hips continued to buck into me. It hurt. It felt good at the same time.

When he came I felt the warmth gush inside me, partly seep out. There was a warm sticky fluid leaking in the crevice between my buttocks, forming a wet patch beneath me. I felt Miguel's dead weight against me.

He stayed like that for a long time.

Gently I pushed him to move.

His head came up first. He slowly moved out of me, now no longer erect. His eyes briefly went to the place between my legs where he had been. He gasped. "My god! You're bleeding."

I had to calm him down. Explain he'd been my first.

He was in some kind of awe of what had just happened. His eyes swam with unshed tears. I made my excuses to go to the bathroom. The

Alisa Miller

burning between my legs was intense and I needed to wash.

I took a long time in the shower, reflecting on what had just happened. I thought to myself then that, on the whole, I had probably been quite lucky. Miguel had been considerate. He had been tender. His alcohol-fuelled confessions had fleshed out the man behind the camera for me and suddenly I was not quite sure if he had really taken advantage of me or me of him.

When I went back he'd fallen asleep. I lay on the bed beside him, feeling the warmth of his body and I thought, back then, just how strange it was to live like this. One place after another, working in front of the camera, selling emotions, looks and images and having no real place to call home.

Alisa Miller

#7

Oklahoma City show, St. Petersburg, Russia.

Flash bulbs go off and blind me. It's the familiar sensation of brightness and black pots. I feel the urge to close my eyes. Resist. I breathe, face set in a mask that projects an image. The catwalk is at least four feet off the ground. I can't see a thing. The lights blind me and all I can think is that I must not slip on the way to the end of the polished wooden floor.

I'm on four inch high heels, a risk in itself and the shoes are half a size too big – potentially deadly. The bikini I am wearing is tiny. I have to move in a way which makes sure the top stays put and there are no nipple slips the press could use. The music sets a pace which is a little faster than what I would consider to be safe. I wonder just how many men are out there, eyes itemising me, cataloguing me for future reference, their companions wondering just what it takes to make the bikini look as good on them as I make it look on me.

It's a game. Always such a game. My job is to make men want me and women want to be me. Women will then buy the bikini or the underwear or the men will buy it for them. The image I have to project is one of bridled sensuality. Lust

Model

Alisa Miller

restrained. Icy and detached, unavailable because of quality.

It's a tall order. The material I have to work with is tiny. A brief scrap around my hips, two triangles barely covering my nipples. The lights are bright and hot but they make the crowd around me vanish into a haze so I don't really complain.

I am conscious of the way my hips move and I know my ass is raising temperatures. I manage to get to the end of the catwalk without tripping up or falling over. One momentary pause as I stand, hands on hips, one leg cocked jauntily, pelvis thrust forward then I turn, make my way back to the end of the catwalk, step off.

"You're running late!" the guy organising us backstage speaks English with a heavy Russian accent and I think it's like being in a bad movie. Any moment now he is going to be unveiled as the mole, the one who needs to be killed by the secret agent working for the good guys. His name is Igor and it only seems to add to the movie-fed stereotype running in my mind.

Backstage the icy calm dissolves into shed clothes, gasps of relief as we take the deep breaths necessary to calm strained nerves and the barked orders as we rush to get into the next outfit in line. My rack has three more bikinis, a bra and thong set and two basques, suspenders and thongs. I have an assistant to help me in and out of the outfits, hand me the next one, take one off me. I am on a really tight timeline here. There is a makeshift curtained booth set up to preserve some modesty but even getting in and out of there makes the process longer so I unclip the bikini top, let it slip to the cold marble floor, bend to pull down and step out of the bottom.

My assistant is fast, there to hand me the bottom of the next bikini first, I notice a couple of men looking my way, wonder fleetingly whether they will be at the party later on, make a mental note to check so I can avoid them. Then time is once more against me. One last check to make sure my bikini top is securely fastened and I am through the curtains and on the catwalk.

**

"Awesome delivery babe," the Neanderthal saying this is Russian. I nod, smile and move on. I remember Brisbane, Australia. So long ago seems like it was someone else's life and yet it has been just five years. The creep at the Riverside Disco handing me his card.

"I know how this looks," he smiled and I noticed, even in the dimness of disco lights and strobed flashes of brilliance, that he had crooked teeth. "It's not a pick up, I am a scout for a model agency. You are just what we need."

I kept the card and, impulsively, three days later, made the call.

Model

Alisa Miller

"We have a client promoting a new range of lingerie," the woman who'd met me had said. I was intrigued because she was a woman, I had expected a man. "It's a cross between angel and demon," she was busy explaining, "We did all the studies and there is an undertapped mistress market, the client has a niche they can reach but they need a certain look. You're it."

There. That's how it had began. I had been hired on the spot and just two days later I was swanning across studio sets dressed in nothing more than sheer gossamer, black lace and satin. After the photo shoot and when the first bunch of pics had come in Anna, who was the manager, had taken me aside and talked to me.

"This is a tough business darling. Make no mistake. It's murder on budgets, goes through cycles of fashionable looks which may find you out of work as fast as you found yourself in work and it's hard on the girls. More than half of those I take on go on to get hooked on drink, drugs and men in that order."

I found her honesty endearing and her intensity interesting and I had asked: "What do you suggest I do?"

"Go on and complete your plans to be a shrink, if nothing else it will at least make sure that your own shrink bills are minimal. Stay off the drugs and use the drink sparingly, it's bad for your skin and it makes your eyes go all puffy. Finally when it comes to men, pick the ones you can control. Don't even go near the ones who might want to control you."

"That's it?"

"That's it."

It made for a totally sensible package of advice and I found myself thinking about her words more and more.

My demeanour at the party afterwards earned me the title 'ice queen' and a reputation started for being distant, aloof and maybe even a little dangerous to know.

Still it's a hard profession to conquer. Anna had been right. Fashion is not just subject to design styles which change every six months, it is also subject to 'tastes' for models which means that unless you are willing to put your body and mind and heart on the line and live so publicly that you become a brand in itself, creating a fashionable taste for you, as it were, you soon drop out of fashion and disappear.

Though I was always on demand the calls that came for me were mostly lingerie, swimsuits and sexy fitness clothes. There were no grand openings using me because the designers were not sure I had the right look for them. They were not sure about that they were getting. They did not know if they could trust me to bring their creations to life by imbuing lifeless cloth with my own persona.

It's a really funny business.

Model

Alisa Miller

The money's good. The travel really messes up your circadian rhythms and, for me, the fact that catalogues and lingerie and swimsuit shoots have longer timelines to those of fashion meant that I could concentrate on Uni in between and make sure that study time missed was made up for by extra tuition.

"Awesome!"

The person who's saying this has a greater degree of sincerity to what I am used to and it breaks me out of my thoughts. I zero in on him and take in the look: pony tail, slicked back, teeth artificially whitened, permatan, shirt monogrammed discreetly on the breast pocket, slacks unrelieved black. Designer or stock broker. I knew most of the designers so I took a gamble.

"Markets still going up enough for brokers to afford good coke?"

His stunned look told me I was right. I had also pulled the carpet from under his feet, reversed the stakes and signalled that I was not your usual model on the pull, all in one go.

"Damn! They were right about you!" he gasps. "Mike, Mike Horness," he offers his hand and pumps mine before I can make any other suggestion.

"They?"

"You are the talk of the circuit darling. Girl who speaks her mind and spends more time thinking than drinking," he smiles as he says that.

"They have odds on me down at your club then?" I ask. The tiny hesitation tells me that they do and he is debating the merit of telling the truth and risking being tainted by association and (probably) participation or lying to me and risk being found out. I have him as an inherent gambler, it is the nature of his job and he does not disappoint me.

"They do and I have a stake in it but if it means losing your company right now I would gladly double it and lose it,"

Interesting take, I think. "How much?"

"Five large ones and counting."

They're betting fifty thousand dollars on who amongst them will sleep with me. It's fluttering in its way. It also says a lot about the backward state of our world. We celebrate youth, virility and beauty and then go ahead and readily put a price on qualities which are not designed to be reduced to marketable commodities. We raise an eyebrow then at models who get hooked on drink, drugs and men in order to cope with a world which idolizes them and then, in equal measure, silently conspires to destroy them.

"Well Mike, I will do you a good turn then as you seem a nice, friendly man," I say. "Double your stake in it for none of them getting any bragging rights to me. Then triple it on no stockbroker achieving this in a year. Commodities are prized for their scarcity."

He smiles and nods. "Can I buy you a drink at least?"

Model

"Alcohol, ah, god's gift to men who want to seduce women,"

He is reduced to tears with laughter and I suddenly find him likeable. Stuck in a roomful of designers whose first language is Russian I find Mike's company relaxing and though I know I will not sleep with him, or indeed anyone he may remotely know, it is comforting to hear one's own language again and communicate with people who do not need to have your syntax translated in their heads before they can reply.

"I suppose you would not be inclined to help me win the bet?" he says this with a straight face and I find that the option does have its attractions. "Split the proceeds with you,"

"So your interest in me is purely fiscal?"

He laughs at that but I also see he is thinking about what I said. "I know you can make more than that in a day," he says, "but it's a changing world. It's good to have some extra money though at the price you'd better be worth it."

I suddenly find him tiring. It's taken all of one minute for him to go from flirty, clever and congenial to boorish, crass and utterly boring. I wonder then if it is me, is there something in me that brings out the worst in those I meet? Do the mixed signals I inevitably send out contribute to them feeling that they can say anything and get away with it?

I am annoyed and then get annoyed at myself for being annoyed. I wonder suddenly if I will ever manage to find a guy who will push all the right buttons. Someone who will make me feel real as opposed to a bitch or a slut.

"Aren't you jumping the gun a little sailor?" I say and his mirth dries up. He has heard the tone in my voice and sensed the anger behind the words.

"I didn't mean anything by it," he starts and I find that even more crass and boring. It's the perennial defence of the indefensible. Why, I wonder, would any right thinking person say something that means nothing? If it really means nothing why say something, anything at all? No. It always means something, they just hope you will agree and then also agree that it did not really mean much anyway.

"You did, but let's get past that," I hear myself say and wonder why I find it difficult to completely belittle them, strip them of their pretences and show them to themselves for the people they really are. It suddenly forms an intellectual puzzle for me which takes the edge off my anger.

The slight softening of my expression is seen and it gets instantly misunderstood.

"You can't blame a guy for trying," he says and tries a winning smile. "Besides you've got to admit we'd be really good together."

I really have no idea how he can make that judgment but I have now lost all interest. "Maybe next trip," I say abstractly and start to wonder off.

Model

Alisa Miller

"Wait!" his hand wraps itself round my wrist and I fight the urge to throw my drink in his face and knee him in the groin. Whenever I can I spend time in the gym, working out, kicking heavy bags. Ballet may be more gracious and maybe the kind of image a model would want but Kick-Boxing is the best thing that can happen to a girl who wants to keep fit, stay interested in what she's doing and get rid of all the stress that sometimes accumulates just by going through life.

I got into it by accident when I went with a male friend once to enrol for an aerobics class. There was this cool instructor. I remember he had this air of calm. I am totally used to gym rats. Male models preen about tensing their pecs and rubbing their abs like this is the magic key that will get us to give ourselves to them. Some of the most insecure people I have met have been male models. After a one-night stand with one I vowed to myself that I would never again have sex with a male model. It's not the one-subject matter they have in terms of conversation: themselves, it is the sense of things being wrong. Somehow we have taken the male body, the sculpted physique, the chiselled cheeks and turned them into a feminized version of beauty.

After sex he'd broken down and cried, shedding hot tears on my shoulder. He found the pressure too much, the rejections too cruel and the passage of time which would rob him of his body and his looks, too difficult to withstand.

Model

Alisa Miller

I was used too to the jocks. The ones who pumped iron and made love with the same single-minded dedication because to them both things were equal. It was, in each case, about them and their performance. The cold metal at the gym was as equal a challenge to them as a naked woman's body. In both cases their solution was the same: go at it hard and do not let up until you are exhausted.

I was used too to the aerobics queens. Ex-gymnasts who now tried to relive the glory through loud music and ultra-competitive, full-house classes filled with chicks wanting to be the next miss tight-ass of the year candidate.

This guy was totally different. There was an easy calm around him. He looked slight compared to the male models and iron-pumping freaks I was used to. He was slim and very compact, with eyes which looked like they could see right through you. And yet he had this air of total confidence about him and he was very polite without being diffident.

I liked him instantly.

"You girls looking for something special?" he'd smiled and I was intrigued. It wasn't so much what he'd said as the way he had said it. It oozed charm and confidence and something undefined that made me look closely at him.

That kind of self-controlled assurance is difficult to come across and even harder to fake. He was the kick-boxing champ and he took the classes. Sometimes I find that the greatest decisions, the ones which will most affect your life, are taken on a whim or a lucky fall of circumstances. Had I not made the decision I did then, had we decided not to go for aerobics but instead just joined the gym, then we would not have talked to the trainer and I would not have started kick boxing and my life might have been very different indeed.

I truly believe the gods above have a sense of humour. They throw things in our path and laugh at our reactions. They change the course of our lives or shape our characters at a click of their fingers. We are like cockleshells bobbing about in a massively wild current called life. We sometimes hit turbulent waters and sometimes we find that things get rough. We dream of a steady ride through the currents or some quite eddies to allow us to catch our breath. The current pushes us ever onwards, pitching us against rocks and other cockleshells and obstacles we have no way of predicting until they are upon us. That's life.

"Don't touch me!" I twist my wrist and slip it away from his grasp applying pressure against his fingers with the inside of my wrist bone. The effect is that my hand slips out of his large, beefy hand with ease and he suddenly realises that he had been holding me and now he doesn't and he does not know how that happened but he knows that I am angry.

"I am sorry," he is quick to put both hands up to chest height, forming a barrier between us, palms open, facing me.

Alisa Miller

"Well Mike, thank you for a nice evening,"

He flinches with the sarcasm in my voice and does not move as I walk away. I exaggerate the roll of my buttocks under the tight skirt on purpose and I know he is now mentally kicking himself.

Outside the sky is dark and the weather has a bite to it. There is a liveried Russian at the door which he has opened for me. He says something in Russian which I do not understand and then he says something in English. About getting me a taxi.

Russia is a strange culture where excess has its own reward. In a country where beauty seems to be everywhere, where women compete with each other on looks and style all the time, models who have made it are given a lot of respect.

I smile, nod, tip him and say softly: "Spasiba."

The taxi ride to my hotel is relatively short, perfectly cocooned. Afterwards, lying alone in bed, naked, feeling my own body with my hands I feel the deep sense of loneliness which has gripped me. The tears which come have a cause which is too deep for me to understand so I just give up to them, cry into my pillow, sobbing until, eventually, the pain washes out of me and I drift off to a troubled sleep.

#8

Nevsky Prospect, St. Petersburg, Russia.

Life is meant to make sense but, I am convinced, just not immediately. The St Petersburg streets simply have to be the most competitive arena there is for women. I am walking through Nevsky Prospect, three-inch heels, and a skirt that's about the same in length. I have a fur stole on top because the Russian cold cuts through your bones.

Russian women have a special way about them which I have always been fascinated by. They seem to have a built-in understanding if what it takes to please a man that's instilled in them from birth, practically. The models I have met have seemed to be out of this world and I now know why.

Walking through the square on my way to one of the most beautiful museums in the world the Hermitage I feel one of many. Wherever I look, blondes and brunettes teeter on heels at least as high as mine, lithe bodies gracefully moving through the crowd. Clothes tastefully put together even if the cost is not high. Eyes made up to shine, cheekbones expertly highlighted. It is like a crash-course on make up and beauty.

It makes me feel strangely exhilarated. Amongst so many beautiful, sexy women I feel vibrant alive, their passion for life infecting me. My phone vibrated just before it rings and I pause to get it out of my handbag. The Blackberry is my best friend. Having lived out of a suitcase for what is now getting to be five years I have made its memory my home. All my contacts and their details and all my life are stored there.

I answer quietly as not to draw too much attention to the fact that I am not Russian. Russia has evolved fast. Each time I work there I am shocked by the advances I see. More shops, more goods, more people. Yet it is still a wild, wild place which can be very dangerous. The cops policing the underground are little above thugs with a badge. I know they answer to no one and the fact that they live in one of the world's most expensive cities and are expected to survive on $250 a month is evidence of a mentality which expects them to supplement their income through blackmail and extortion.

There is a sadness inherent in a situation like this. The beauty of the city and its people juxtaposed against the system governing their lives and keeping them locked in mire. It is a contrast which is not lost on me. It makes me feel both sad and angry. I am sad because I know that no people, as a whole, can ever be made to evolve unless they are ready. I have been on photo shoots in Cuba at a time when the average Cuban made up the daily calorie ration he needed to survive by chewing on sugar beets. I have been on photo

Model

Alisa Miller

shoots in the Dominican Republic when we needed a discreet armed security guard in our hotel, for safety, and when, right next door, in Haiti, thugs with machetes walked the capital's main streets at night delivering their own brand of 'justice'.

I have seen the desperation which comes with the realisation that they are missing out on something and have no idea what to do in order to change it. I am angry because I know Communism, that great idea which in order to work requires saintly people, has held them back for more than 50 years.

My life and my work is a paradox. I live to provide a sense of the unreal. I work in a way which highlights and promotes the very excesses of our civilisation which I find least attractive.

The thought makes me realise just how deeply lonely I have become. I know it does not do for models to become too introspective. It's like actors, musicians and rockstars. You suddenly realize that the very vehicle you use to make a living is the thing you should be railing against. It makes for a dichotomy of thought which makes you 'difficult' to work with.

The thought processes make me sound distant on the phone and my interlocutor hangs up and I find, as I walk, that I have already forgotten what he said and what we talked about. Like a girl in a fairy tale I let the St Petersburg streets suddenly claim me, forgetting my intended trip to the Hermitage. I flow with the crowd, going from expensive shop to expensive shop. I look at the

Alisa Miller

displays and look at the clothes and look at the prices and in window shopping I put together, in my head, a very clear idea of how fast things move, of the disparity between rich and poor, of the effects consumerism has on a society which for many years had been locked behind an Iron Curtain.

I notice some glances from some passersby but this is the part of St Petersburg frequented by people who do not need to ask about prices so their glances are casual, curious. There is no danger.

The walking, the window shopping, the energy of the crowd and the sense that I am a kind of forensic explorer, analyzing what I see at a much deeper level than usually possible, works its magic on me and I suddenly begin to feel alive again, excited at being here. I think of the steps which have made it possible, the journey I have taken and the man whose unfaithfulness made me feel so lonely and so alone and I vow to myself to never again get so attached to any guy. It's simply not worth it.

The Blackberry vibrates again and I pick up before it can ring.

"Ali, where are you?" Mitch's voice sounds far away and suddenly so familiar that it brings the well of tears behind my eyes. It's an unexpected response and it catches me by surprise and I really, that moment, do not know how to react, or what to say.

Model

Alisa Miller

"Mitch?" it sounds so lame and I know it.

"No it's Santa,"she says and she makes me giggle. "Where are you girl?"

"St Petersburg, we have one more day. I am flying back tomorrow."

"Met any Russkie princes?" I laugh at that. "Though more likely you become a gangster's moll there,"

"I am nobody's moll Mitch,"

"Oh, feisty. Love it. You ok?"

"Yeah, just the city getting to me. Too Russian," it's her turn to giggle and she does. "You had a call, that's why I called you."

"Real estate?"

"No, some creep wanting a photo shoot. Some Miami media baron launching a new lifestyle magazine. They saw, apparently your New York lingerie pics and their dicks perked up," Mitch can be really crude at times.

"It's just work," I say.

"I know,"

"Tell them to call,"

"I did. This is the heads-up so you know."

"Ok, Mitch, thank you,"

"You are welcome darling. Take care and stay cool, ok?" she makes me smile with her style.

"You too."

The line goes dead and I suddenly feel homesick. I feel tired of the travel and the uncertainty. Tired of the false happiness and the smiles which hide less honourable intentions. The entire modelling scene makes me feel tired and jaded and as the feeling sweeps over me, unbidden, in my mind comes the night before.

I was just getting back to my room from the gym. The gym had been empty, no one around. I was sweaty, the lycra shorts and cropped top wet. The towel draped over my shoulder, hair tied back in a pony tail to keep out of the way.

The elevator door has slid open. I had a business suite, all to myself, another girl's Monica, was next to mine and as I turned to go, there was a man at that door. Dark haired, slim. Wearing an expensive suit.

My mind had freeze-framed the scene. The door opening just wide enough to admit him. Music and laughter coming from behind. Monica in something short, hair in an elaborate display, up. The guy slipping in and, in a momentary glimpse, someone else, blonde, unknown. Long hair fanning on her shoulders, naked.

Then the door had closed, as quickly as it had opened.

Each world has its underbelly.

Retail shop assistants steal stuff from the store room and sell it on eBay. Financial advisers take advantage of rich clients and feather their own nests and pharmacists write prescriptions under the counter for extra cash.

Models....well, models. I guess when you live by your looks you tread a very fine line.

I blink to clear my mind from the vision I had glimpsed and decide that maybe it really is

Model

Alisa Miller

time to get out. The Miami shoot will be my last. I promise myself that and, determined now, I turn away from the shops and the bright lights and in the cold St Petersburg air I head away from Nevsky square and towards the Hermitage and Russia's famous cultural treasures.

#9

Palace Square, St. Petersburg, Russia.

The Hermitage started almost by accident. Like much of Russia it was the dream of just one person. Catherine the Great, apparently purchased some Dutch and Flemish works. She needed somewhere to house them and that's how the entire thing began. I knew that from history lessons at school but nothing had prepared me for the sheer grandeur and beauty of the buildings' exterior.

The State Hermitage, as it is called, is all about history. Its ten buildings breathe Russia's cultural past inside and out. I allowed myself to become lost in it. Blend in like a transparent person. This is a trick I learnt when very young. Modelling is all about projecting. Inside our heads there is a mental switch. Crank it up and something happens. Like a search light going on.

I have tried to understand how or what without much success. I just know that when I have to I crank up this mental switch and it's like I have suddenly turned a beacon on. Those photographing me seem to suddenly connect with me. If I am on a catwalk those who are watching me sit up suddenly and take notice. I have the ability to make an entire room stop and stare just by walking in, switched on like this. I learnt, early on, that this works both ways. Crank the switch down to its lowest possible setting and it's like a powerful search light has suddenly been switched off. No one sees you. I have travelled on buses like that, unnoticed, listening to people's half-conversations, watching the way they dress and interact and it was like I was made of glass. No one paid the least attention to me and I felt safe in my invisibility, protected.

Inside Russia's rich history I find myself becoming transparent. Tsars and Bolsheviks, peasants and emperors, hovels and palaces. Look deep enough in any museum and the past comes down the great hill of time, its echoes unravel, its guts spew out and what you hear is the cry of men and women and children, each trying to make sense of what is happening as time and history rush through them.

We are never more than wisps in the eyes of time. Mere shadows and in the Hermitage I felt a sense of my own fallibility, my own mortality which was at odds with the opulence of the place.

I stand in one of the white rooms. I let everything go through me. The time and the place.

"Madame Alice?" the voice disturbs me. I open my eyes.

"Yes,"

He is tall, gaunt in a stereotypical fur hat with the flaps turned up. A big heavy overcoat on his frame. For a moment I feel disorientated, transported to a spy film. I am a double agent. This is my KGB handler.

"Lieutenant Sergei Lanov," he introduces himself smartly and I shake his hand, the spell broken.

"Yes, how can I help?"

"You do not remember me Madame," he says, "I was in charge of hotel security at your fashion show,"

I nod. I am annoyed that I do not remember. It was a stressful day and I had been focusing on what I had to do and I did notice the security men. The realisation annoys me because I never want to think that they are invisible.

"I am sorry," I say.

"No Madame, no need," he is apologetic in a way which I find endearing. "I was told by the hotel staff that you headed this way,"

His words filter through and I am annoyed that I have failed to become invisible. Eyes watch me wherever I go, noting what I do, what I wear, how I walk. I suddenly long for invisibility.

"Yes,"

He shuffles a little awkwardly and lowers his voice a little, his accented English heightening the sense of conspiracy. "There has been an incident at the hotel madame," he says, "we are asking all the models questions,"

"Incident?"

"Yes, I am sorry. I would like you to come back with me to your hotel."

Model

Alisa Miller

He has a car waiting outside, and a driver. When I enter they put on the flashing siren and we head back towards Nevsky Prospekt. It occurs to me, in the car, with two men I have never seen before to think that I never asked for an ID, I never questioned who they were. All the horror stories of the Russian Mafia and its singular ability to abduct rich foreigners come back to me.

I wonder if I should say something. Do something. My mobile phone is with me but to take out now and make a call, to whom? Where? I dismiss the thought, trust my instinct.

The little car goes through St Petersburg's busy streets, slicing through the traffic with an abandon which I consciously refuse to consider. It does pull up outside the Radison SAS hotel and the gaunt guy in the fur hat rushes to come round and open the door for me.

Inside, in the lobby, there is pandemonium. More guys in fur hats, some in epaulets. Some models milling around. Guests. And guys in suits, I recognise the accent and realise they are British Embassy staff.

"What's going on?" I ask one guy nearest me. My Russian police escort seem to have melted in the background. I can't seem to find them, a minor talent I decide, no wonder I did not notice the guy at the fashion show.

"There was a death," he says, turns and looks at me, his lips purse. "I am sorry, your name?"

Alisa Miller

"Alice, I am here with the fashion show, what death?"

"One of the models, in the suite. Looks like an overdose or an allergic reaction to something, we don't know."

"Who?" I ask and I can hear the shrill tone in my voice.

"Sveta Boshinova," he says and I remember the glimpse I had of laughing girls, the door of the suite closing and the music fading. Death, it seems, manages to creep everywhere. Ruining the fun of life. The name of the girl rings no bells with me, but somehow I cannot shake the image I had of the laughing girls, the guy closing the door. It all seems so wrong. To die so young when there is so much to live for. It all seems senseless and the thought infects me with a sadness which I suddenly cannot shake.

We are ushered into one of the hotel's conference rooms where the Embassy staff hover anxiously as the Russian police ask questions. I answer honestly telling them all I know. Then it's over, everything as meaningless as before.

Later in my room, alone, I watch as the Russian sky outside begins to snow, its white flakes floating from somewhere high and alighting upon everything, covering the Earth in a mantle of white and, in the darkness of my room, without reason, I begin to cry.

The tears burn deep inside me, they sear my soul, bring up a pain which I had to fight hard

Model

Alisa Miller

to suppress and which I can no longer hold back. My own failed relationships, the struggle to stay afloat in a world that seems to be designed to drag you down, the heartache of betrayal by lovers and friends, the crassness of strangers coming on to you because you are a model, it all builds up into an undefined, overpowering wall of bitterness and pain and it rears like a wave above me and then comes crashing down upon me and I let it.

The sobs tear through my chest, the unknown girl's senseless death, triggers the emotional flood which sweeps through me and I let it. I feel the need for the catharsis which follows, the need to purge everything which has been building up inside me for some considerable time now.

The tears streak down my cheeks and make my mascara run and shake my frame as I sob and I hug myself because there is no one to hug me and I feel so alone that it hurts and I almost wish to die. The realisation of this shocks me. No one should feel that way. Something is terribly wrong with the world. With me. The loneliness which creeps in then is like a knife. It makes a part of me deep inside go chill and then the chill spreads until my teeth are chattering and the shaking I experience is as much a part of the sobbing as it is of the cold that starts from inside me.

I really want to hide. I want to crawl under the blankets and blot out the light and melt into the darkness. It's primal and it's instinctive and it beckons. It appeals and I almost give it to the temptation there and then and do it but I catch a glimpse of my reflection in the window and I stop.

We are all two people. One is designed to function in the world outside. That self keeps responsible jobs, goes to meetings, is creative, obeys the law and tries hard to help those in need around it. That self is logical, civilised and, given half a chance, highly cultured. It lives by professed belief systems and never subscribes to anything which is not subject to analysis and careful thought. That self is a recent development. I think of it as a coat. It sits on top of us, covering us completely and it gives us whatever shape it is designed to do: baker, doctor, street-sweeper, model.

Just like a coat it does not comfortably sit upon us for long without suffering extensive wear and tear. It needs to come off from time to time, hang up to breathe. Brushed down, dry-cleaned. That's when the real us, the ancient, atavistic manifestation of all our illogical fears, beliefs and hopes is revealed. Our logical self knows that getting a job promotion, winning a race, getting a new boyfriend is the result of activities which have nothing to do with rabbit foot charms, favourite racing tops or lucky lipstick colour. Yet we do all of these things. Our illogical side runs deep and manifests itself in many, different, small ways.

Sitting up on the bed, in my hotel room I see a reflection looking back at me whose roots trace back to a past which was old when the Earth was still young.

I am afraid of myself. I am afraid of what the slick, professional model will ask me to do as part of her logical drive for success. I am afraid of the world which is so huge and so indifferent that it can snuff out a life and call it an 'incident'. It is these fears which look back at me now from the window pane reflection and in understanding all this I get angry and anger brings determination.

Radison SAS has a small conference room. Fully equipped, projectors, web, VOiP and cameras for web conferences. It's a hotel. It has a system. Things need to be booked in advance, prepared, paid for.

Money talks everywhere though and provided no laws are broken or no reason supplanted, things can be made to work. Rules can be bent. Things can be made to happen faster than the system allows.

I talk to the concierge. I talk to the duty manager. I then talk to the manager. Some money discreetly changes hands. A credit card is charged a certain amount. The room is booked. I have an hour. An hour before I then have to get back to my room and start to pack. I am determined that I will not be packing and again heading into the unknown.

My Blackberry has all the numbers I need. I start to make calls. One is to my agent. One is to a publisher I met at a party last year, the next is to a publicist. The key to understanding how systems work is to understand why they work.

Publishing is a business, like any other, and it runs on a system, like any other business. Those who are outside it think that publishing is there to serve the public (information), to provide entertainment (art), to enrich the world (culture) or to create an additional stream of infotainment (celebrities). The truth is that while many of its facets involve just such an activity it is there to do one thing only and do it well: make money.

Publishing is an industry which hides beneath many facets. It couches everything it does in terms of risk and it then goes into a working model which is designed to minimise all risks and ensure that each book published provides a profit. Worst case scenario that profit is slim. Best case it is so huge that it dwarfs even Hollywood blockbuster movies.

It does this at the expense of the author. It does it subtly, pervasively and consistently and it can get away with it because publishers hold all the strings. If you have a book and you really want it published you have no choice. You need a publisher and the publisher is, always, in a position to dictate their acceptable terms of acceptance.

I knew all that. Once, in Madrid, after a photo shoot and the obligatory party afterwards I had slept with the son of an old Spanish family who had made their fortune through publishing.

Model

Alisa Miller

The night was young and we were both hyper and in between hot, sweaty, exciting rounds of sex we talked, and talked and talked about films and books and culture and publishing and film-making and modelling as a profession.

"If you are really interested in getting a book published you need to guarantee publicity,' he's said. "Publishers cannot resist a morsel which is wrapped in publicity. Free publicity is the best kind. Paid for publicity is the next best thing. Publicity however is expensive. Publishers will never pay for it unless they happen to have a cert success in their hands and that happens only once in a blue moon, which explains why there are so few good books published and why established authors can have massive marketing campaigns publicizing average books which yet go on to become best-sellers. The public buy into the publicity. The publicity machinery provides sales, sales become big news. Everything then takes its own predictable course." He'd smiled and reached for me, predictably, I thought. And I'd let him, losing myself then in the moment.

The words had stayed with me. I had his number still.

Long shot, maybe, but one worth taking.

The phone rang,

Twice.

"Yes?" his slightly accented English made him sound like Inglesias. I remembered why I had fallen for his charm the first time.

Alisa Miller

"Carlos, it's Ali. Long time." The pause told me he was adjusting, recalling details, deciding what to say.

"Ali, my god! Long time right. Where have you been?"

It's a good start and I get the pleasantries rolling. Time, place and where I am at.

"St Petersburg? My god, you hate the snow." He remembers and it's all good so I take the conversation to the next level.

"Carlos, you are plugged in for a video feed?" I ask.

"Yeah sure," he gives me his Skype address. It takes a few minutes to get plugged in myself and project his video image on the big, presentation screen. "God Ali, you look awesome," his schoolboy expressions amuse me but right now I am too focused to become annoyed by them. I smile to show I acknowledged his compliment.

"I am thinking of writing a book," I start and see him nod and perk up in his seat a little. "Something backed by a bikini photoshoot in Miami to launch," the Miami thing is pure improvisation. I am entertaining the possibility but have not yet worked out the details. I know however that Carlos will need to assess the publicity in order to tell me if the deal can be done.

If he remembers the fact that he had told me what gets publishers excited he gives no indication. His eyes, face and body posture however show that he is hooked. Excited. I explain some of the details, the kiss-and-tell part, the introspective part, the mix between salacious details and hard-working advice.

He is hooked. He leans forward staring into my image on the screen on his desk and makes suggestions, comments. His hands are gesticulating. He smiles a lot.

"So you think it will work?" I finally ask.

"Ali with you on the marketing front shooting bikini shots we could sell aspirin recipes in a leather-bound volume made from the dried-up old skin of thousand-year-old mummies and it will still sell," he says.

I laugh. It sounds funny. Part of me also notes the cynical fact: packaging sells. Never mind the content.

"Ok then," I say. I am now ready to take things to the next level. I need Carlos to give me a contract without having to sleep with him. "I have an offer from Beetleman's I just wasn't sure how to best assess this and needed an insider's ear," I say.

Beetleman's are a big firm based in Washington. They have a tradition of bringing books to the public which break the mould and become best-sellers. The last one they did was *The Samurai Diet*. A diet book based on the supposed eating habits of the legendary Samurai, written by a woman who had spent her childhood in Osaka learning to be a Geisha. It had gone on to sell three million copies worldwide.

"What? That idiot has made you an offer?' Carlos is sitting up staring into the screen.

I can't lie. But then again I can't let a good opportunity go to waste. I stretch the truth a little knowing I can then hide behind the chain of people.

"My agent has been bandying around the idea of a novel for some time," I say, "the Miami photo shoot deal is coming up and Beetleman's heard about it," I tale off not wanting to go deeper into something which may later put me in a difficult position. I let him fill in the blanks on his own.

"Has he said how much?" he asks taking the bait.

"Carlos no. You know what they are like, my agent is negotiating. Until he gets the maximum possible I am kept in the dark."

He looks at the screen and through it my eyes thoughtfully. I sense he is thinking about something deeper, making a decision which is not entirely his to make. I am about to put him out of difficulty by saying let's think about it and closing the connection when he, having finally decided something, leans eagerly forward, his voice dropping a couple of notes.

"Ali, this is hush-hush," he begins, "we are about to take over a major English publisher. Two-hundred-year-old firm. They are in trouble but have a solid backlist. The deal's not done yet which is why this is all hush-hush but if it goes through then this kind of book might be the perfect vehicle to start a new direction, use their existing network and reputation with English outlets."

I understand nothing's concrete his end either. I think about it. Make a decision.

"Carlos, I will keep this open then. Give you first refusal at it. Do you have a date?"

"Four weeks," he says. "In four weeks I will know. Can you hold out that long?"

"Ok,"

"Do you want to come to Madrid at some point to discuss this face-to-face?"

I am not sure just how much of this suggestion is business and how much his sudden need to see me. I can see that on the screen his eyes are cloaked a little. I decide to play it safe.

"We shall see. I have assignments all over the place at the moment. They need to come first. Do you want to see an outline of the manuscript? A sample at least?"

He waves his hand impatiently at the screen. "If you can write one millionth part as good as you look we are onto a winner he says."

It annoys me. Looks in writing should play no part. It is neither the moment nor the place when I change the world however so I move forward from there. "Ok, I will get you a sample once I am back in London," I say.

He smiles. "Sounds good Ali. I will be in touch. Let me send you my new email."

"Ok, Carlos. Take care."

The click of the connection cutting out plunges the conference room into silence. I realise that it has taken me just forty minutes to get everything moving my way again. The chime of my Blackberry tells me that a message has arrived. I check.

It's Carlos' new email. I check it quickly. He has not resisted the impulse to put in his new title: Acquisitions Director.

Men. If it's not the flashy cars and fancy mansions, it's the new titles. Still, I say to myself, women use clothes and make up, lipstick, hair and low-cut tops to get what they want. So it does balance out.

I realise I need a laptop or a netbook. Something with a little zing to it. I have started the process after all of getting a book contract and have not even written a single line yet.

On my way to my room I stop by the information desk and enquire about where I could buy a laptop. The clerk there is obliging. He makes a few phonecalls looking for the best place to help a western girl who doesn't speak Russian get a good deal without getting ripped off.

Five minutes later he has an address and has booked me a drive with the hotel's car.

On my way up, in the lift, I suddenly feel like a huge weight has lifted off my shoulders. Life seems to be bright again, full of promise and possibilities. It took t close brush with someone else's mortality to snap me out of my self-indulgent sense of pity. I suddenly long for the kiss of decent Miami sun on my back.

#10

Heathrow, London, UK.

Heathrow. It's always the same. The taxiing of the plane down the runway. The wait while some unseen things are put in motion and then the opening of the plane doors. Smiling pilot and stewardess saying goodbye. The dry air and the snap of cold of the ramp as we exit into the chute that will take us into the airport itself.

There are cameras watching you all the way apparently. Experts profiling those who might look suspicious. I have flown BT, taking one of the more expensive flights from St Petersburg on purpose. It means the crowd is less Eastern European and delays are less likely. It's totally wrong to profile like this but it's the way things work. Fewer security delays and less likely that someone is smuggling in something they shouldn't. On paper anyway. In reality the only difference between the people on my flight and those flying Aeroflot lies in the disposable income they have and has nothing to do with character, belief systems or personality.

We are all accidents of birth and products of our circumstances. Had I been born in Cuba or Nicaragua or a favela in Rio my fate would have been decidedly different to what it was now and the issues of survival facing me much starker. All of this I know instinctively. It makes me grateful, each time, for who I am and it makes me determined to become even better. Knowing how many millions of others on the planet are struggling makes me determined to take nothing for granted. My looks and my place of birth are something which I could not really control. What I can control, however, is what I do with them and the choices I can make which will take me further.

Before a plane lands I go through a personal routine. I re-touch my lipstick. Check to make sure my make up and eye-shadow are perfect. Spray on a little perfume. It's a small ritual of self-affirmation. It makes me feel better about myself. I know that during landing, just like during take-off, is the time when the plane is at its most vulnerable. Pilot error, weather conditions or a flock of pigeons getting sucked up by a turbine can contribute to a crash. I cannot control any of that and, realistically, I do not think the way I look as the plane destructs would make me feel any better. I have spent so much time in the air that I am convinced that should the time come to get married fertility might be an issue with all the radiation I have absorbed over the years. I know the odds of having a crash and the complex systems the technology of our civilization puts in place in order to avert it. Yet I still cannot help this little atavistic personal ritual.

The chill of the ramp gives way to the warmth and lights of the airport itself and the thought hits me that all these years I have been

Model

Alisa Miller

getting on and off planes without anyone waiting for me at the other end. Vulnerability works in weird ways. You can go through a war zone perfectly detached, feeling that you are just an observer in a movie, the misery, pain and death around you leaving you untouched, the possibility of your own violent death remaining an unentertained notion at the back of your own mind. A photographer friend who did a stint in Beirut told me he never once thought that he might die or get injured and the only way he could connect with the things he was photographing was through his viewfinder.

Or you can become unbalanced by the smallest incident. A tiny pebble setting off an avalanche in your psyche which destroys the balance of your foundations and leaves you vulnerable to oscillations which can undo you.

Perhaps Ray's infidelity which now felt to have been so long ago was the pebble that did it for me. I felt myself unmoored, set loose upon an orbit I had no control over. Heathrow felt empty to me, cold at a deep, psychological level I could do little about. I waited for my luggage and went through customs with little more than a standard check. The smile of the person at the security check made me feel unusually warmed.

"Was it cold in Russia?"he asked and there was the hint of flirt in his voice.

"I am glad to be home," I smile back and the way he straightens and gives me back my passport made me, irrationally, to want to suddenly hug him.

Outside it is raining. The customary London drizzle. Black cabs are lining up and I take one, the cabby's burly presence becoming yet one more of the elements I am using to make myself feel cocooned, safe, loved, wanted. I look forward to seeing Mitch's familiar face and smile.

***

"Darling that sounds awful," Mitch's concern is always touching because I know it comes from the heart. "To die so young and so pointlessly," she has made lasagne, my favourite and we are on our second bottle of wine. Her flat feels warm, cosy. Safe.

"I know," I say, "it makes us all think how lucky we are,"

We have been talking for hours and the good food and the drink and the warmth have worked their magic on me. I have already showered and changed and we are lounging in the living room, in front of Mitch's huge, fake, electric fireplace. I am busy telling her about Russia and my plans and the death of one so young and why I think men are pigs and Carlos and the possibility of giving it all up and starting to write for a living and she is listening.

Model

Alisa Miller

Mitch is the perfect listener. She never misses a word you say. She asks questions which are intelligent and she never fails to be sympathetic. The lights are off and the heating is on and the flat feels as warm and safe as a womb. Mitch keeps filling my glass up and I regale her with my experiences of Russia and my plans for the future.

"You know I would really miss you," she says and the huskiness of her voice makes me realise just how much I need a friend, need to feel that I am more than a face in the crowd.

What happens next is the result of the wine and the fatigue of flying and the good food and the warmth of the flat and the fact that I am tired, truly, deeply, bone tired of feeling lonely and alone and at the mercy of fate. Mitch's hand is on top of mine, squeezing it gently, her fingers, warm, strong, tender, caressing the back of my hand.

We are sitting on the rug, on the floor, our backs against the heavy leather settee, facing the beautiful dancing flames which never tire nor fade and thinking, each in her own way just how lucky and yet how lost we are. And Mitch turns and leans forward and her lips caress mine.

It is a flutter, like the beating of a butterfly's wings. Her lips feel warm, dry and then her tongue, moist and pointy, playful and yet shy, enters my mouth, seeks mine. It's difficult to explain to guys about this. Girls enjoy the closeness, the intimacy and the togetherness that sex can bring in a way which I do not think guys can. For them it is all about the mechanics. The release. It builds up inside them to the point that they cannot think clearly and they then simply need the mechanical release which acts like a safety valve inside them.

With girls it is all about a shared journey. The touch, the scent, the process it becomes something which, psychologically, takes us somewhere else, a place where we share strength and intimacy as well as pleasure. It's a process which leaves us feeling better than before, unplagued by questions and untroubled by insecurities.

I feel the whisper of cloth as Mitch sheds her clothes and mine begin to come off. Her tongue on the tips of my nipples is insistent, urgent, her hands, strengthened by sculptor's work the moulding and plying of clay and the shaping of marble and stone are running down my back, feeling every single ridge of my spine.

Like an instrument my body curves to her touch, my breasts thrust out to be suckled, my pelvis thrusts forward. Her head is buried between my breasts and I seize her hair in my hands, pull her head up, find her lips and in the desperation born of loneliness, and the pain of feeling lost, I plunge my tongue down her throat, desperate, urgent, seeking to get past the physical barriers and connect; make the shared physicality of our bodies turn into a mind-meld. A union which goes deeper.

Model

Alisa Miller

"Relax, relax" she breaks off the urgent kiss and whispers down my ear.

We are on the floor now her hands tagging gently at the thong of my panties, pulling them down my legs, past the knees, to the ankles where I carelessly kick them off. The glow of the electric fireplace adds an atavistic primitivism to what I feel, what we are doing and I abandon myself into the moment, lose the loss and the loneliness, let go of the pain which is the result of too much thinking, too much rationality, too much analysis.

I cry out involuntarily as her fingers, insistent, deliberate, delve inside of me. Find a spot where I am sensitive. Play a primitive game there. My back arches, I gasp. Her hands pull my legs apart and I think just how hot her tongue is against me. The seconds turn into minutes and the minutes turn into hours and neither of us really lets up.

Mitch has been hungry. Wanting this way too long. I have been lonely. In this mutually passionate grip I feel nothing but pleasure, the ebb and surge of passion, feeling and a deep sense of love.

I am all over her. Mitch has a slender body. Legs which have the fullness of a woman. When I turn her over and press her head down, expose the curve of her neck for me to feast upon my fingers are inside her already, exploring her in every way, leaving nothing untouched.

It's this breaking down of barriers, the sense that there is nothing separate, nothing apart, no part which we cannot touch, taste, explore which creates this sense of total abandonment, the breaking down of the individual and its remake into something else which transcends civilization and takes us back into a time where all we were, all we could be was a mass of sensations.

I am stronger than her, though I am slimmer. I hold her down with ease and her cries of surprise and pleasure feed into my own feelings and sensations. When I let her go she turns and her hands cup my breasts and need and her legs wrap round my waist and she arches her back so that her pelvis and her shaved sex rubs fiercely against me.

"Darling, again, please again," she gasps and I smile a feral smile and have barely the time to think that it's going to be a long night.

It's sometime the day after the night before. I try to take stock of where I am. It is Mitch's bedroom and I am in her double-bed though I have no recollection of how I have got here. There is a nude on one wall. A grainy black and white reminiscent of the early days of photography, though the model's trained body and clean lines of limb tell me that it's modern, the grainy noise the result of Photoshop filters and photographer's work rather than age and time and technological limitations.

Momentarily I think that this is what we do these days. Use our technology to go back in time. We use advanced digital photo-editing techniques

Model

Alisa Miller

to make our photographs and portraits appear dated and full of 'noise'. We use the best of wines and fatigue to shed civilization, go back into a time when we were primitives inhabiting caves, using our physicality to procreate and pleasure each other because life itself was all too brief and too uncertain and procreation was all we had in order to ensure survival.

My thoughts are interrupted when the bedroom door opens and Mitch comes in with a steamy mug of coffee. It smells good. As she bends over me I think so does she.

"Afternoon," she says and smiles.

I thought, should anything like this ever happen it would be awkward, it would destroy our friendship. I feel good. Drained. Somehow remade, as if the draining took away all the bad things inside me and gave me only the good things to hold onto.

"What time is it?"

"Two o'clock. Your agent rang, twice, some jerk wanted to speak to you, once, left no message. Some guy wants to know about a casting call, they are looking for models to feature in a documentary about models making careers for themselves, it was from the BBC, details on your Blackberry apparently, I gave him your email. Then some other jerk called, Russian by the accent, wanted to know where you were." She was smiling as she said that.

I touch her hand. She is dressed in jeans and T, no bra and her nipples beneath the top bring back vivid memories of last night. She bends and kisses me lightly on the lips first, then the top of the head.

"Two o'clock?" I gasp.

"Relax, you needed this."

"Last night..." I was not sure what to say.

Mitch smiles. "It was what it was. No regrets and I know that this does not change anything between us. Besides I needed this too. Been working under pressure too long."

At that moment I think I could grab Mitch and kiss her and hold her forever. What have I ever done to deserve a friend as good as her?

"Branch?" she asks and I nod.

"Need to shower first,"

"Bacon, eggs, salad and fresh bread?"

I think how the bread is going to kill my diet. I try to stay mostly on a protein diet. I know how models are supposed to eat just lettuce leaves and some seeds followed by a glass of wine or two and that's not far from the truth. I know girls on the circuit who are constantly hungry, their bodies under immense stress all the time. There is a body-fascist trend in the industry which demands that we are not just thin but as thin as possible. I have always fought against it. I have shunned smoking as a way of keeping the pounds off and used my gym sessions to maintain my weight and my one sacrifice has been carbohydrates which I keep to the barest minimum.

Model

Alisa Miller

I have not eaten bread for the best part of a year but I feel really special this morning and Mitch's offer is too good to turn down.

"You're on," I say and leap out of bed, totally naked and unembarrassed and head for Mitch's shower.

#11

The Barbican, London, UK.

I never cease to be amazed at our capacity to experience the world through specific moments. A sunset at sea, soft rain falling in the spring. A special dawn reflected off layers of snow. All of this imprints us in ways which we do not, indeed cannot, readily analyze. It imprints us and makes us special and makes us different and then what is left is something new. How we choose to synthesize the experiences of our lives is the special path we take which then leads to events we experience.

There is a danger here that we see this, somehow, as being such a personal construct that we are directly to blame for everything which happens to us. Certainly we are the architects of our own fortune (or misfortune) insofar as the fact that we are the only ones who can make the choices necessary at key moments. No one else. But that's only at the nexus points, the points where we actually have a choice we can exercise. Once that choice is made we are passengers of fate, mere observant, watching the scenery of our lives unfold, until we get to the next point of debarkation, the point where we again get to choose what to do (and what not to).

Model

Alisa Miller

I am thinking about Miami. A place where fresh hope and broken dreams live side by side. I had spent some time there once, living with a friend whose apartment in Coconut Grove was one floor below J-Lo's.

"The problem with her," he'd said, "is that she's trying too hard to not be a Latino." He'd said this with his back to me, staring out of six foot tall windows looking towards the sea and the boardwalk running alongside the beach and I could not tell, at the time, whether his voice meant this as a good thing or a bad thing.

I left two weeks after that. Deciding that the occasional bout of angry sex and the novelty of living in an upmarket Miami address were not sufficient compensations for putting up with weirdness. The thought and his words echoing now in my mind suddenly bridged the gap of time between the me, then, and the me, now. I felt that somehow I had learnt something then which was applicable now.

Was there something wrong with not being yourself? As a model I became several different people each time I worked. The wanton, the bitch, the sexpot, the child, the woman. These were faces I wore with ease, putting them on and taking them off as each outfit or photo shoot required.

Did J-Lo know who she was? Was it something she did not like and was trying to remake? Who was I?

The thought, like a crossbow bolt, cut across my train of thought, stopping it short.

Making me sit up and think. I am, still, in London and it's raining outside. I feel the innocence of the person I had been when I first heard those words in Miami and that person has now been changed. She's seen death in people she knew and known casual sex and the violence that often goes with it. She'd seen promise snuffed out like a candle because there was no sense of hope attached to it.

She thought she had found love and had had her heart broken. She had felt her own sense of ambivalence looking into what passes for beauty in the mirror and had resisted the urge to smash her face against the glass, destroying the looks behind which hid a carefully crafted sense of anguish.

We are all so complicated. And things are simple.

"Ali, you ok?" Mitch's sleepy voice next to me makes me aware that it's early. My body clock is out because of the travelling but I guess it's about three in the morning.

"Yeah," I say and fall back in the bed. Mitch is half asleep. She throws an arm around me and her hand snakes across the flat of my stomach. It stays at my belly button, fingertips lightly caressing my skin, bringing up an electric sensation which finds an echo in my nipples. I feel the familiar tightness of excitement at the back of my throat as I anticipate what's going to happen next.

Model

Alisa Miller

Mitch's hand trails downwards and I open my legs to accommodate her as she finds the centre of me. She is gentle, prying, insistent. She has short, rounded, smooth fingernails she files carefully and I feel her fingers ease inside of me.

"You feel so good," she says and begins to slowly move against me. Her head comes off the pillow next to me as she repositions herself and her lips dart across mine, then dive for a hardened nipple.

It's the lateness of the night I tell myself. The thoughts of passing innocence and missed opportunities which had been firing across my brain. The sense of urgency which has suddenly gripped me, a sensation that life is flowing fast, much too fast for me to stop and I need to really sample all of it. I grab her head and press it against my breasts and Mitch obliges her tongue darting across hardened nipple tips, her mouth opening to take me in.

Her fingers, in the meantime, sleek with wetness, have found that special place where all the sensations of a woman reside and she is busy toying with me, fingertips rubbing. My back arches involuntarily, my body responding against anything I may think, or say or do and then all thoughts seize to flit across my brain as intense pleasure takes hold of me and I am lost, lost, lost in the searing white heat which flashes against my closed eyelids.

Lost. I am lost.

***

It's much later and Mitch is out. The night's excesses have drained me and I feel cast adrift. My life not entirely my own. The Blackberry buzzes with email messages I am not going to check today. I feel like I have reached a nexus point. Too many things have happened too fast and it's a sign that I need to change something.

Modelling used to be my life. I followed the trends, travelled wherever they might call me to be. Put on any kind of attitude necessary to sell the clothes. I played roles in my head which projected a personality, 'the beauty', 'the bitch', 'the spoiled child woman', 'the waif', 'the classy girl', 'the athlete', it had been fun but now I could feel the weight of all those personas inside me dragging me down. It is not fun any more.

I can almost feel the tears in my eyes. The burning is there but I now feel dry, like something inside me has changed fundamentally and I am not yet sure how to assess it. I know I need to do something but I am not yet certain what that should be.

When I feel like that I do one thing: I find ways to destroy myself, break down the barriers and reduce the person to a heap. It is something which is latent in each of us. I have seen it in models before, the slide towards drugs or alcohol, the binges and the drying out. The histrionics and the pendulous swings. The orgies and self-destructive relationships. They all happen for the same reason: we are unhappy with who we are and want to discover a new us and in order to do that the old self must go.

Most times we fail. Drugs, alcohol and sex have a habit of becoming the end themselves rather than the means to it and by the time we realise that it is usually too late. The process has taken its toll and the person, in trying to become more real, has been damaged. I am not immune to the need but my drug of choice is different. I use exercise. There have been times when I have stayed on the treadmill for hours, lungs burning, legs gone rubbery, vision starring in front of my eyes and my body shivering with exhaustion even as sweat ran down my forehead and blinded me and all just so I can feel reborn, my angst ran out, my uncertainties evaporated along with my energy reserves.

I know that this is what I need to do now. Now. I feel the need, the urge and I need it.

It is much, much later and I am in the shower. It's late and I am not alone. Mitch is pressed tight against me, the hot shower water needling into both of us as we move against each other. Sometimes we get lucky with the people we meet, the friends we make. We meet people whose needs are filled by what we have to offer and they sense the loneliness in us and it is these people who then manage to connect and take us into an entirely different dimension where words are totally superfluous.

Mitch does not speak. The bathroom is lost in steam and the water keeps needling on us, making our flesh rosy. Tongues and fingers and hands and teeth lick and enter and fondle and nibble and it is like we are both locked in an intricate dance where each step, carefully balanced, hurtles us towards some unseen edge.

My body exhausted from the treadmill work and the press ups and the sprinting aches and tingles and arches as Mitch, on her knees now uses her tongue on me and I throw my head back, eyes shut against the cascading hot needles shooting from the shower head above us and I feel like I have finally lost control and I open my mouth wide and as the hot water shoots down my throat I let out a guttural gasp.

It is much later, dry and sleepy, pressed against each other, drawing warmth from Mitch's body against mine that I whisper in her ear: "Thank you".

She's mostly asleep. She nods and presses against me harder.

She does not yet know it but I have already decided. There is a photo shoot I need to do tomorrow – a promo shoot for a new range of thigh-highs. What my agent calls quick and dirty money and then I will head for Miami and the opening of the fashion collection there.

Model

Alisa Miller

Outside Mitch's bedroom's window pane the London weather is a customary drizzly but it is with the blue skies and bright sunshine of Miami in my mind's eye that I fall asleep that night.

#12

Albion Towers, Soho, London.

"Ok, now walk this way," the photographer's voice grates on my nerves. He has a twang which I find irritating. The traffic and the drizzle have combined to get me to a job feeling a little edgy and the place does not help.

He works from home, like most of these small-time guys. His apartment is above and the studio is downstairs in a typical West London loft conversion, about six floors in all. Try to take any kind of decent photograph in London and you know you need to fake the sun and use the kind of high wattage light inside which makes your models' bodies melt.

I've been modelling thigh-highs all morning walking on three-inch stilettos, trying on different outfits and styles looking to create a variety of looks which will fit in with the magazine's multi-cultural readership.

'Bent back, a little darling," I oblige almost on autopilot. I have forgotten his name and his make up artist has gone home as we are nearing the end of the day anyway. All that's left is now me and him and his assistant and the click and whir of his camera. He still uses film which I find an oddity but I have worked with luddites before in this

Model

Alisa Miller

business and I have learnt they are a breed unto themselves.

The assistant's name is Luke and he can't be older than twenty. His eyes are glued on my legs and a couple of times, as I changed in and out of outfits I caught his reflection on the mirror as he passed by the door of the small cubicle that passes for a dressing room in the photo studio. It has no door, not even a screen but it's turned towards the far wall and there's not much call for anyone to be there as all the equipment is on the other side of the room.

I am used to the creeps that hang around shows and shoots so Luke is not unduly worrying to me.

The lights are really hot though and I have not had anything to drink since breakfast. There is music in the background (there always is) and champagne on offer but I have declined that. I feel dehydrated after yesterday's hard run and hot sex and I just want to get the job over and done with.

It takes two more hours.

By then my feet ache and my back is sore and I am thinking that if I see another pair of high-heeled thigh-high boots anytime this century it will be too soon.

"You look tired," the guy's twang cuts across my train of thoughts.

"Yeah, rough night," I smile.

"You can grab a shower upstairs before you brave the London traffic," he says and suddenly I feel that a quick freshen up will make the drive back more bearable.

I dress light for photo shoots and I always take a robe and now, as I thankfully get out of the boots which have been killing my feet, I wrap a black satin robe around me. I am dressed in thong and low cut bra, the shoot went through the entire range: 40 pairs of boots and as many changes of clothes and styles, ranging from vamp in underwear (the last one) to kitten in pink skirt and bolo top.

I take my duffel bag and sling it over one shoulder and pick up jeans, trainers and top and head for the stairs.

"Shower's first door on the right just before the bedroom," twangs the photographer and I smile and nod. My mind is already on Miami. I know I should call Neil, my agent quickly to let him know the shoot's over but I am tired and I really want to get back home.

I find the shower. The guy has style for sure. The bathroom's one huge wetroom, Soapstone walls and tiles throwing a soft green light and a massive, opaque window letting in the sickly London light. The water, when I turn it on, is like a lover's caress, washing away everything that's weighing down on me today.

Sometimes things happen by design and sometimes they happen by accident. Opportunity and poor judgement combine to create situations which logically should have never happened.

Model

Alisa Miller

Later, much later, when my head is clear and I can think about things again I will blame myself more than anyone else and get angry because I let fatigue and stress and a grey London day get to me and take away my focus. That would be later. In the wet room, as the water cascaded down I was still in a place in my head where those thoughts had not yet happened.

I turn the water off and reach for the towel and I suddenly become conscious of the silence. Until I had got in the shower I was only aware of the need to feel fresh again, get in my car and drive home without feeling the pressure of having to rush. Now, I become aware of the fact that I am in someone else's shower.

I wrap the towel tightly around me and on bare feet pad out of the wet room. The music downstairs has stopped. The day is getting on and the grey light coming in from outside seems particularly forlorn. It imbues a sense of urgency in me.

I had undressed in the bedroom. My clothes are there and I hurry to go and get dressed.

I become aware of them almost immediately.

They are both in the hallway outside the bedroom. The door is wide open. The edge of the bed I can see framed from this angle seems like an open invitation to a madness which suddenly looms large in my mind. I cannot see their faces clearly but the stillness makes me realise that the booze they have drunk is working on them. They are in the process of being changed from men to rutting animals. Alcohol and the presence of a woman are working to push them against the barrier of reason and then beyond.

Self preservation kicks in. My blood pressure shoots up, I can feel the throbbing in the veins at my temples and I can hear my heartbeat deep in my ears. I know that if I run it will provoke them and then things will get out of hand. There are two of them and kick boxing training notwithstanding two against one are never good odds.

The choices available to me leap in my mind with frightening clarity – stretch into timelines with a predicted ending. Some of them involve violence and death. Others end up with me on that bed, the plaything for two booze-fuelled oversexed men.

One or two present me an alternative ending.

I take a deep breath. Let it out slowly, stand on the balls of my feet, force my leg muscles to tighten, then relax as I slowly come down on the pads of my feet again. The movement forces awareness back into my body, makes the madness of panic recede. I need to be calm for this.

"Nice shower," I smile and walked towards them.

The expression of uncertainty which flashes across their faces emboldens me. They have not expected this response. I suddenly take courage, realise that I have more than a chance here.

"Haven't been in a wet room since Miami when my agent booked me in with Swimsuit World for the cover shoot," I keep my tone casual, neutral. Willing the message to cut through the horny craze in their brains and get through to the higher processing centres.

He is a professional. My agent knows where I was. I need him to think, understand before I am forced to spell things out and give them the opportunity to take the chance.

"You like it?" he asks at last.

His voice is tight with lust, tension. But he does not slur his words and I allow myself to feel even more hope.

"Yeah," I am almost upon them, realise I will have to walk between them to get to the bedroom. I play the scenario in my head, think of the angles. I was not going to go down without a fight. If they want me, if they were intent on taking me, they will have to kill me.

Sometimes decisions are made without logic. Sometimes logic dictates actions which are not acceptable. One course of logic, now, clearly said that if I wanted to survive all I had was to give in. Let them use me. Get through this and come out the other side. Sex, is always preferable to violence and maybe death.

I understand logic.

Logic said that they are professionals. They have a reputation which has to remain intact so they can continue to make a living. They will not want to do anything to damage this. Logic dictates that they should not try and force me.

I have to make then realise it.

I reach them. Ready for anything, prepared to strike out, run in the bedroom and use anything I can find there as a weapon.

"My agent will call you tomorrow to discuss the option of working on an offer basis," I say. Offer-basis are options for models who work through photographers. Photographers are usually hired to photograph models. They are subject to the tough contracts magazines and fashion houses put in place. As such their costs are pushed down as far as they will go and as far as a market full of supply will command.

Some did the clever thing. They managed to work with models on an offer basis. If a shoot became available or an opportunity presented itself the photographer would take it and suggest the model as he would have one ready and waiting. Because the model came with the photographer the deal was cheaper. It made sense but it trapped you into constant work just to get to the same amount of money as when you did the big gigs which asked for you by name.

I see his eyes widen as he tries to process it. His cohort, untouched by this, is still intent on me but I am watching him closely, guarding for a move but not really expecting one. He will take his cue from his boss.

Model

Alisa Miller

Sure enough he stands his ground, suddenly uncertain, his eyes darting to his boss.

"He will?" the photographer asks. His mind is suddenly weighing options, thinking about money.

"Yeah. I called him a few minutes ago, before I leapt in the shower. He will call you back," I say. I am at the bedroom door, then through it. I have made the world intrude, forced it upon the two Neanderthals and made them realize that they are not working in a vacuum, now I have to seize back control. "He has a lot of magazine contacts," I stop then, inside the bedroom, and turn back. I am inside the bedroom door. I know I can react faster than they can move but even a closed door only buys you a little time. Determined men are hard to dissuade. "If he likes your work, thinks he can work with you he will be able to get us both the work we need."

It is the clincher, I see the light change in his eyes and I know I have connected. I have switched over at that moment. From being prey I have gone to being with him, on the same team. Now he can see a future where magazine gigs are lining up to book us both.

"I need to get changed," I pointedly close the door. Behind it I wait listening for a moment. Something is said which I cannot make out and then there is the sound of the two men making their way downstairs. I wait listening for another five minutes and I hear, thinly, the sound of music coming up from downstairs. I breath a slow sigh of relief. I have talked them down, on my own. It is high time to get out of there.

The drive home takes place in a surreal fugue where possible scenarios and what if timelines run themselves in my head. In some of them I end up being raped, in others I show up dead. I somehow feel it significant that I had got out of a situation which had suddenly turned hostile, as I had. It is a sign.

Most people think that it's easy being a model. You make money from being photographed, living off your looks. As you might expect the life of a model is far more different than most people think. There is the pressure to look good. As a model your face and body are your assets. You invest in them in food, which most times is as little as possible, and cosmetic products, which are always expensive, and drugs, which for most models become part of the lifestyle, and therapists, because neuroses are unavoidable when you live in an uncertain world where trends may make your looks obsolete and where time is totally against you.

Taken as a whole the entire existence of a model is based on an artifice. On society's need to feel forever young and healthy and carefree. Few models ever get married and fewer still have children. Few models commit themselves to one man (or woman). Few models manage to survive their career psychologically intact.

Model

Alisa Miller

When you think of the profession you're in, in those terms, funny things happen in your head. I had had close calls before but never something like this. It angered me that though I had read the situation correctly there was nothing I could do. Nothing had happened. Those two idiots would be free to put the next model through the same scenario and that girl may not be as lucky as I was, or know what to do.

I drive through the drizzly London roads, battling with the traffic, thinking that this was no real way to live but failing, at that precise moment, to really see any viable alternative. Like most people I long, at that moment, for the protective arms of someone I love, someone to love me. I really need to feel safe again, protected. Stop feeling like a girl alone.

It is a thought which suddenly feels like a stake spiking through my heart.

I am, at the moment, alone.

The realisation hurts. Brings tears to my eyes and I bite them back.

A black BMW swerves from a side street, cuts in front of me. It shocks me back into the present and suddenly I feel alert, like I have been pushed back into my body, no longer seeing and feeling from a distance and I feel this frightening imperative to now simply get home, safely, and crawl under the duvet, isolating myself from the world.

The thought occurs to me that from the outside looking in I must seem hard, self-contained, successful and, in reality, I am more fragile than an eggshell. I have been travelling far too long. Working on my own for what seems like forever.

I feel the need to get out of Britain, stay, for once, under skies which do not rain every day.

First, though, home.

#13

Albion Towers, Soho, London.

The lips on my breasts are strong and insistent. A darting tongue teases out my nipples, the lips then surround the tumescent flesh, suck urgently upon it and I feel the tingling fire inside me which makes my back involuntarily arch and a sigh escapes me.

Strong hands have seized me. They slide down my body, to my hips. Cup my buttocks and I surrender myself to the sensation, something inside me finally gives. I want then to lose control, to let things go, to belong, fiercely, to someone whom I trust.

The passion unfolds and takes me over. A kernel inside me wants to understand. It peers incisively, closely, through the fog and the darkness and the searing physical sensations which make me feel like a doll gripped in something much bigger.

The strong hands play my body like an instrument. I yield.

I feel a strong knee between my legs. It roughly parts my thighs.

I am naked.

The sensation which follows next sends a white, blinding light to explode against my eyelids

The part of me which was looking then reacts.

I sit up.

The flat is coolish. My chest is heaving.

I never sleep with underwear on and in the darkness my breasts are rising and falling, in the twilight seeping in from outside the window my nipples are painfully erect.

I was dreaming.

"You ok?" Mitch murmurs beside me. Her hand, sleepily snakes under the bed clothes, across my hips. It stays there, suddenly comforting and I lie back.

It was a dream. Dream. It was so vivid.

I work in a profession which takes sexual imagery and promotes it to an art form, subliminally projecting sub-textual messages of sex appeal and desirability, all linked up to clothes and hair and make up, designed to make objects sell. I have, as a result, have always had a healthy, logical approach to sexuality.

Sex is good. It can be enjoyable. It is necessary. Nearly all the things, I think wryly, relationships should be and aren't.

I very rarely fantasize. When I do, I am always alone and I have a toy and the mood is upon me. I have worked with my body all my life. At school, growing up I was fascinated how in gymnastics, or dance or athletics, my body had to be trained to perform. It had to be taught what to do. Later, as a model, I was fascinated by the fact

Model

Alisa Miller

that the pictures I have in my head, the mental imagery I project, has the ability to substantially change telltale markers on my body and the way it moves and holds itself.

I could be the 'the Madonna', shy but confident, beautiful but innocent and my body would project a picture which on photo shoots would look so much more different than when I became 'the vamp'. Everything we are, I think, is a potent mix of mental and physical images, subroutines which themselves unlock a whole lot of mental and psychological states.

The 'berserker' in battle makes sense and is effective exactly because this happens. It is the same in modelling.

I understood that at an early stage and taught myself to be versatile. The swimsuit Alisa looked different to the lingerie Alisa and both looked different to the girl who would go out shopping in the morning. Yet each of those was me

Lying, in bed, in the dark, staring at the ceiling, listening to Mitch's sleepy breathing I found my mind racing free. It was like I had suddenly become disembodied and had found myself floating in mid-air. All I could see was possibilities. The sudden horror of the almost-incident with the sleazy photographer and his assistant, in the Soho apartment, came into full focus then. I had a vivid image of myself naked and held down, legs forced apart as they took turns on me. My will to resist exhausted. My body now totally not my own.

Alisa Miller

I saw, in my mind's eye, all the long string of choices which had led me down this path and the possibility and I resented my ex boyfriend more than ever because he had had such a hand in it. I felt alone, unprotected, very little understood and –in his case – betrayed. Everyone I was around of or had contact with seemed intent on taking something from me, asking for something, giving very little in return.

It should have made me feel angry.

It made me feel incredibly lonely and very, very small.

I started to shiver.

***

"Sounds like post-traumatic stress to me," it is morning and John Lewis Oxford Street provides a beautiful backdrop of style, efficiency and quality service. I look at Neil, my agent, seeping expensive coffee, sat across from me, and I wonder if he really seems me as a person or as a means of making cash only and the thought itself is so uncharacteristic of me or the way I normally see Neil that it frightens me about the person I am becoming.

"Do you think I should do anything about it?" I ask and the question itself sounds ridiculous. When you suffer from an illness you get help. You don't debate if you should.

Model

Alisa Miller

He misunderstands my question. "I will put the word out on the circuit about him," he says, "He will find it hard to get more work. Without evidence however proving anything else is going to be your word against theirs and they are two,"

Yeah. Two. They were two yesterday too. I let it slide. I need to focus on my plan to get away from Britain for a while. A stylish shopper crosses my field of vision over Neil's shoulder. She's dressed in skin-tight denim jeans, cashmere boots, a white ballet top with a deep V at the front and a tanned jacket with tassles going down each sleeve. She's in her early thirties, her face just beginning to get the look of the mature woman, a hint of loss of freshness on the skin.

Her hair is drawn back into an elaborate knot. Blonde with curling ends.

I wonder then, looking at her, as she pulls up a chair, sits at a table and looks at her watch if she really has a life as perfect as the image she so successfully presents. The bard had it right. The whole world is a stage. We each have parts to play in it.

"Ali?"

I refocus on Neil.

"You're daydreaming," he says without rancour and it softens me. The fault is that I expect him to be more than an agent all the time. I expect him to be a friend, a confidante, a mentor. He does all that but only within the boundaries of our professional relationship. That's good, I think with sudden insight, because he has never come on to me and it stops him from over-stepping the boundary. It means I can rely upon him and he has always been there when I needed him.

"Tell me about Miami," I say and the sudden relaxation in his shoulders makes me realise how tense he was. He ha fully expected me to say no.

"Peach of a job, peach. Two weeks' gig, all expenses paid, full set up. Magazine stylists, photographers, everglades locations sans crocodiles," he smiles at his own joke and I have to smile back.

"Swimsuit or lingerie?" I ask.

"Both. You're doing the swimsuit shoot outside, the lingerie stuff at a studio. All fully attended," he hastens to add and I realize now why he had been so tense.

"Money?"

"They are paying everything upfront, taking care of the expenses. Anything you need while you're there is on their tab."

"Sounds mighty decent of them,"

"It's a good gig," he sounds defensive. I lean across and touch his hand.

"It's ok. I said yes,"

"I know Ali. I am not saying-" he stops. Looks at me for the first time since we met. There are dark rings under my eyes. I have not slept much. The night has been spent thinking. I have picked clothes which make me feel comfortable rather than elegant. Caterpillar boots and jeans. A white blouse and black leather jacket. No make up. Hair pulled back in a pony tail. Face scrubbed. "Are you ok?"

"Yes,"

"Are you really ok?"

I consider just how much truth I can safely inject into the answer.

"I feel a little lost Neil I am not sure if I enjoy what I do any more."

"That's understandable you know." He is suddenly sympathetic. "It's taken some time for you to get to this stage. You have made a name for yourself now though, it's right to start thinking about picking bigger jobs, saying no to all these crappy gigs. I have been thinking about how we can do this."

He takes my silence for consent.

"Big gigs need a brand more than just a hot looking girl. They need a persona to go with their product. Think Kate Moss and her bad girl rep or Hurley and her suppressed passion and resentment look." He is talking about gigs which could be worth millions. "I have discussed it with a couple of contacts. I can get you hooked up with Barrington or Jimmy Rattner, arrange for the paparazzi fanfare which will follow, exposure across all majors," the names are big families in Britain, one connected to the Royal family. There would be a press feeding frenzy.

"Hooked up?" I enquire.

Here he pauses. "This is the catch Ali. There is always one and you know it best. These are playboy types, head up their own arses. They're not going to agree to take you out and start a paparazzi storm just to better your career."

Yeah. I would have to sleep with them.

"It's not like they are abominations," he says, "there are plenty of girls who would die to be able to step out next to them,"

"I know," He is right. Here we are, in the 21st century, living in one of the most advanced cities in the world and I have to sleep with someone in order to make more money and advance my career. I wondered if it was any different 10,000 years ago when I would have no choice but to sleep with the best hunter in the tribe in order to make sure that I had regular food. It suddenly seemed wrong to me and I was annoyed because I was, apparently, the only one who thought this way.

"Anything I should be concerned about?" I ask, playing the game, hiding my anger.

"Jimmy, I hear is into bondage," says Neil, "likes to be tied up and shagged senseless,"

Great.

"Barrington is into partying hard,"

"Wasn't he involved in the air-stewardess scandal?"

"The one about sex in the first class section?"

"Yeah,"

"Yes, that was him."

Splendid.

Model

Alisa Miller

"And you think I will get bigger gigs?"

"Ali," he says, "you've got the look. You sound great on interviews. You just haven't got the rep. Those looking at you have nothing in their heads to make you stand out from those other thousands of pretty girls who would drop on their knees and do anything to just get a foot in the door,"

The imagery he conjures up is suddenly very unappealing. I find myself thinking of going back to counselling, starting a practice maybe, writing the book I have been talking to Carlos about. There must be other ways of earning a decent living which do not involve having sex against your will.

"You know I really wish it was different. When I first got into this business it was all about the looks, the attitude, a willingness to work hard. These days it has gone all funny with celebrity culture and brat-pack behaviour influencing the public which in turn influences the results of the market research which then influences, in turn, the idiots making the model hiring decisions. Sometimes I get up and seriously think about quitting."

"I'll think about it," I say and the really frightening thing is I am not lying. I really will think about it. "How quickly can you arrange Miami?"

"You leave day after tomorrow. Is that quick enough?" he asks and I smile back my thanks.

***

It is later. Much later and the taste of coffee from my meeting with Neil is now long gone. I take a simple pleasure in shopping. You might be tempted in thinking it's because I am a girl, but it is more than that.

We live in a world which is based upon consumption. In order to drive that consumption forward we devise, constantly, new ways to buy and new reasons to spend. In fashion it's 'the look' what you wear and how you wear it has more than just the ability to make you feel good. It also sends out a complex message about your mood, your income, your position in the world, the place where you live and the kind of person you are.

I know it sounds complicated. That's because, like most 'simple' things we do, it happens to be very complicated. The way we choose to adorn ourselves has a long-standing tradition with primitive connotations in it. It represents a large way of how we see ourselves and how we do what we do. As a result we invest a huge amount of our personality in it and the way we see who we are.

In looking at trends in shopping, new products coming out, clothes and furniture, I take a simple delight in decoding the progress we make and the trends we develop.

Clothes, this year, for instance have incredibly short hemlines. A dare for women who always struggle against time and our modern diets to look more than just good. Furnishings, which for a while, were going along the artificially minimalist now look much more personalized. Less functional and a little more futuristic. Curtains have become thinner and more exotic, reflecting a look and quality reminiscent of muslin.

In each of these I take delight. Looking at things on sale I see a microcosm of our world. A new juicer tells me of lifestyle changes and trends in organic farming, dresses so short that they are a challenge to wear let me know that our world is advancing so rapidly and is becoming so secure that we can focus inordinately on hedonism and frivolity, expanding energy which otherwise would have been spent ensuring basic survival needs.

It is a mental game I engage in which takes me out of myself and allows me to savour the moment, feel alive and grateful for everything I am and everything I have. Back at Uni my professors would often comment on the ability we have to deconstruct our world and see, in our creations, the sum of the histories of the creators: "Take a donut and see it for what it is. A lump of dough with a hole in the middle, the missing part conferring greater value somehow. The value going up precisely because we are getting less not more but in that 'less' we create an identity of something which is truly greater than before."

When I shop I take a delight in what I see and what it means.

It makes me happy.

#14

BA Flight BAW207 to Miami.

On the transatlantic flight to Miami I felt like I had burnt my bridges behind me and cast myself adrift and was taking a huge chance based on a dream.

There are times when you feel that you have to go with your instincts and those times are always when you are at your most desperate, your most vulnerable and cannot trust yourself any more and, incredibly enough, like a conspiracy of the illogical, the things which make the most sense are the ones which are the least logical.

I spent my last day in Britain changing my world.

I spent twenty minutes at HSBC's branch talking to an international bank account manager. I explained I planned to be away for a long time. I needed an account which could travel with me so that my cards were not blocked the moment some sleepless, vigilant, piece of programming spotted withdrawals on my card made in Miami and charges on it made in New York.

They were helpful. I'd banked with them for six years and I had an impressive earnings history. They made sure I had all their international numbers and they could get in touch with me. My lack of permanent UK address presented a problem but as it was a transient phenomenon I arranged for Neil to be my base. He was going, at any rate, to be my constant anchor in Britain.

My next stop was Ray's apartment, what used to be our apartment, my base in the world. I had had a copy of his key made long ago when I'd first moved in and we decided to live together and in cleaning I had come across it.

I had stopped by Sainsbury's and bought some bleach. The apartment was empty, Cherisse was at work and Ray was probably at some meeting. At 11.10 in the morning the block of flats felt eerily quiet. It was a weird feeling, standing there in what used to be part of my world and noticing the small changes and new smells. All the telltale signs of someone else being there now.

At that moment, there and then, I had almost gone to pieces. My new-found resolve suddenly dissolving and me, collapsing on the floor in a heap, sobbing against fate and gods and the unknown. A last minute waiver and then I got a grip on myself and went into the bedroom. The wardrobe door creaked a little as always as I slid it across and Ray's expensive suits neatly arrayed next to Cherisse's clothes brought the steel back in my will.

I moved briskly and business like. I took his suits out one by one. Arrayed them all on the bed. Piled Cherisse's clothes on top of them. All of

Model

Alisa Miller

them. I next went through her drawers, pulled out lacy underwear, thongs and panties, all her bras. I placed them on the bed also. Socks, stockings, ties. It all made a pile which almost invited a match, except I was sure the building's smoke detectors would go off and little of value would be accomplished by a fire.

The Sainsbury's bag I had brought with me contained two 2 litre containers of thick bleach. I unscrewed each carefully and then, liberally, poured it all on top of the pile of clothes, watched with a certain sense of satisfaction as the bleach started soaking in, eating its way through colours and fabrics, begin to work all the way through the delicate materials making its way for the bed and the mattress.

I must have stayed still watching it for about ten minutes. Colours had began to run by then and the room smelled of the strong disinfecting smell of the bleach itself.

By the time I got to Mitch's the removal company I had hired to come and pack some of my things was there and she was going frantic.

"Where will you go? Where will you stay?"

I could not really tell her. Mitch had been my mainstay when I needed it the most and she deserved a lot more than just a goodbye. The thing is I could not stay with her and the crossing of lines from friend to lover had hay-wired my brain. I needed to be alone, think clearly. Decide my own fate in the world.

My call to Carlos almost brought her to tears. "You gonna take up with some Spanish jerk?" she screamed.

I could not really explain. I made the deal fast, arranged for the book contract to be sent to Neil who would look it over and forward it to me.

I spent an hour trying to calm Mitch down, explain to her that what I was doing was for the best. I needed the space and the change. Modelling was killing me. A chance to use my knowledge and training to help others and maybe find a deeper me was good.

"Something to drink?" the air-stewardess' soft, smiling voice breaks me out of my revere. The flight from Manchester to Miami is barely seven hours long and I do not fly first class as a matter of course. I have often wondered why and what it says about me that I choose to blend with regular people rather than seek to isolate myself in the expense of the first class compartment.

This time it has been an exception and I am trying to decide just what I should be doing with myself.

"Some coffee and a bottle of mineral water," I say. I need coffee to keep me sane. I am addicted to it the way other people are to cigarettes. I know that I can go an entire day without food but not without coffee. The headache and short-temperedness its withdrawal has on me is designed to drive me nuts.

Model

Alisa Miller

When you fly you lose moisture. A lot of it you lose through your nose and mouth as you breathe. Cabins are hot, humid places and your body tries to keep your core temperature balanced. Much of it you lose through your skin. Coffee, for all its ability to keep you alert also dehydrates you. Add to the fact that there is also another mechanism, something which we do not know about yet but which kicks in when we cross time zones in the air and which seems to use up our body's stored supply of electrolytes and you begin to understand why frequent flying can leave you feeling punch drunk, with a head like you've spent months partying hard.

I discovered, early on that if I drunk enough water on a flight, anything up to a couple of litres, then I could weather the effects of dehydration and time zone shifts without batting an eyelid. I had, more than once, flown from London to Tokyo, got off the plane and gone straight in a photo shoot without feeling, even, the need to take a quick hotel break.

These are survival mechanisms. I developed them as I worked because they helped me survive better. On the flight, now, I felt like I was slipping between the cracks of two worlds. My practical, logic driven approach to life had failed me. The man I had chosen to spend my life with had betrayed me and my professional life seemed to be leading my down paths which were more and more dangerous, designed to soak up my energy, give little back except cash.

Alisa Miller

I remembered the words a friend had given me once. It was still the beginning of my career and we were together on a Littlewoods shoot in Cuba, shooting swimsuits and lingerie in Winter so they had the shots in time for the Spring Collection.

We were getting changed in a hut by the beach, the temperature, despite the sunshine, low enough to bring goosebumps to our skins and the water outside freezing and the hut walls themselves were less than perfect.

"You think they are spying on us?" I asked. We were naked, jumping out of one skimpy swimsuit into another.

The girl, whose name was Eva, looked at me. "The camera crew guys?" she asked.

I nodded. The cold was making my nipples hard and the swimsuit tops had to be carefully positioned as a result.

"It's the profession sweetie," she said. "We are in the business of selling clothes by making them look sexy and we are the ones who add the sex appeal to the fabrics. Our every move is designed to stir them up. If they're not spying on us we're not doing our job right."

I thought about what she'd said. "We are here with them, anything can happen."

"Yeah, I know. In this job you walk a tight line. Exude sexuality, work it up but try to control the fallout."

Model

Her words stayed with me on every job after that. Control the fallout. Basically we stir the hornets' nest and hope we don't get stung ourselves. It was something which I had managed to successfully do all my career as a model. The close brush I had had with those two idiots in Soho had left me shaken, confidence in my own ability at a low ebb.

The psychologist in me recognised the symptoms, the hard to explain sense of anxiety, the weird dreams and behaviour that was on the edge, for what it was: post-traumatic stress. I was in a bad place in my head and needed to work it out.

"Can I have a little more water please?" My voice polite, steady, professional, as I talk to a passing stewardess makes me wonder at our ability to function at so many different levels in so many different ways. It makes me wonder though whether the compartments where we keep all these little selves of ours were as air-tight as we think they ought to be. Maybe a little of what's inside each compartment seeps out and it contaminates the rest.

If we are, each, a melange of something which is made up of parts kept separate maybe, with time what's inside those compartments mixes with the rest until you no longer have a vessel containing several different parts, air-tight containers, each holding its own peculiar mix, but you end up, instead, with a brand new type of mix which forms a new person.

Alisa Miller

Maybe that's how experience changes us. Maybe that's how we evolve. Maybe that's how we end up who we are which is different from who we started out being.

The thought makes me sadder. I am not sure what I am becoming. I just know I am changing. To occupy my mind I focus on the job ahead. Miami Dade County special, a magazine tycoon who is launching a new concept: news with an edge laced with sex that sells. The magazine has a swimsuit section and they need an outsider to feature on the cover as a strong message that they are different.

Some agency is handling everything there. For me, right now, there is little to do but sit back and try very hard not to think.

#15

Tene Centre, Miami.

The agency is top class.

I am met at the airport by a hunk in aviator sunglasses and a navy blue Jersey. He is holding, at waist level, a stencilled sign which reads

"Alice?" he enquires. He has probably seen modelling photographs already.

"Yes," I give him my hand. His handshake is dry and firm.

"John," he says, "I'm your driver," in one smooth motion he takes my suitcase, bends and picks up my holdall. "This way, I have a ride ready."

It's Miami. The heat is welcoming, the set up buzzing with a glitz which I love. The 'ride' is a stretch limo with the obligatory tinted windows. John is tall, muscled like a bodyguard, with shoulders that stretch the navy blazer he is wearing and a walk which shows that he can handle himself.

The limo is huge, of course, and at the back there is piped music and a fully stocked mini-bar. John sits himself in the driver's seat and turns round to talk to me before he puts up the partition. "The mini-bar has everything and there is even some mineral water there Miss," he smiles a perfect smile.

Alisa Miller

Miami is a place where appearance is all that matters. The city rebuilds itself every five years to maintain property value. Apartment blocks which in any other part of the world would stand for centuries are brought down and put up again in order to keep up the investors' value. It seems wasteful but it drives construction and it drives properties and it drives a city where to be old and destitute is the worst possible curse you can imagine.

Cocooned in the limo with the AC on and a song by Queen piping through the speaker system all this feels a million miles away. It is so easy to think that it can't touch me, that I am OK, that I am impervious to the world and its issues. I know it's not true. We are all good at creating self-delusions and believing in them.

I had wanted Ray to be the one. The real thing. I had wanted this so badly that I had stopped questioning and had started accepting and it had got me to a place where I was left completely shattered, left with no protection and no self-esteem. Spiralling towards some unseen doom which I was powerless to prevent but which I could nonetheless sense.

I have a belief in life which, every time I test, has never failed to prove itself: We are, each, the architects of our own futures. The makers of our fates.

It's not the same as saying that bad things will not happen to us or that there will be no

Model

Alisa Miller

clouds in our little blue sky. These are external factors, things which we do not control. They happen, because they can and they happen when you least expect them to. That bit no one can control. The gods are always determined to piss down on us from a great height. What we can control is our reaction to all this. What we do when things go bad is what determines what will happen to us.

One 'little' thing, however bad it may be cannot destroy us. The destruction often happens because of the things we do when something bad happens which affects us deeply.

I was determined to stop myself from spiralling downwards.

Miami was going to be my last job. In the safe haven of the limo planning a life ahead without modelling seemed surreal, detached from reality. The thought makes me aware of how much circumstances can influence our mindset and our decisions.

Modelling is a glitzy lifestyle. There is an ephemeral quality to it which attracts girls because we know that our beauty, by nature, is ephemeral. The lights, the parties, the drugs, the sex and the money combine to seduce us. Rob us of the reason which drives most people until we are like wild flowers there to be picked and used up and thrown away the moment we wither.

Sad? No. Real. It's the way it is.

No one forced me to go into modelling. It came about because of the way I look. I studied in tandem with my modelling jobs because I do not want to be just what I see in the mirror or on the cover of magazines. In life we all have a choice and the moment we have to make it we realise just how hard it's going to be. It's at that point that we decide whether we want to go ahead and take the journey awaiting us or hold back and become almost-runs, those who could have been contenders if things had been different. 'What-ifs', those who did not do but think they should have. I have met people like that. I have seen the sadness in their eyes and I have heard the bitterness in their voices and I know that both the sadness and bitterness stem not from what they did not do or what they did not achieve but from the fact that they did not try and by not trying they did not get the chance, the opportunity, to discover what they were made out of.

I vowed early on in my life not to become one of these people.

Win or fail. Live or die. I vowed to always try.

In Miami I am now trying. I am putting my life back together again. I am making decisions which will take me down new paths.

***

Model

Alisa Miller

"Take your clothes off in there. We shoot on the balcony to start off with." Clipped Cubano accent and the neutral tone of the professional.

I am in a plush apartment that's obviously used for shoots and shows. Everything is top class in it. Decked out with the expensive taste and style of the interior decorator who knows what the public wants to see.

The place where I undress is one of the bedrooms. The bed is massive with a headboard made of black leather in a room that's bigger than many apartments I'd lived in. Carefully laid out on the bed itself are the wisps of fabric which pass as swimwear. In a little smaller pile, next to them, are three sets of see-through bras and thongs. The underwear shots which, I guess, will most probably happen in the bedroom itself.

I take off my jeans and T, unclip my bra. Undressing for photo shoots in countless locations has stripped me of self-consciousness where my body is concerned. For me it is an instrument I use in my profession. I know how it looks and how to move it so as to make it look more appealing.

Photo shoots are always about being in the zone. In my head I become the part the role requires.

The wisps of fabric tell a story. I know the designer is ex-Cuban. Someone who swam over with a group of friends ten years earlier and landed illegally in Miami. The swimsuits are revealing but as I look at them I also see something else. There is a yearning here. The designer is using a woman's body like a canvas. He wants to make it look sexy but he also wants to make it look natural. He wants to make it tsand out but he also seeks to make it belong.

There is a dichotomy in his design which makes me suddenly realise that what I see is filtered through my psychologist's training. I see the designer's investment of himself in this and I feel a pang, deep inside. I also know what he wants. I know what will work best.

When I come out of the bedroom, wearing wisps which look ready to dissolve the moment water touches them I feel like a wounded goddess. I project the hurt and sorrow and passion and desire and deep, deep inside me, the sane part of me which thinks modelling is a crazy profession, sees and understands and explains in a quiet voice which I choose to ignore that my moment in life makes me, somehow, perfect for this one job. Now.

There is a momentary stunned silence.

I notice the eyes of the light grip boys glaze over with a film of desire and the male response is noted and brings an inward smile in me which never reaches the outside.

The photographer clicks his fingers imperiously. He's recognised the moment too – he galvanises everybody with a single look.

The rest which follows is like a carefully choreographed ballet. The light grip boys sweat and contort and into almost unimaginable positions as I move about the terrace. Pose here.

Model

Alisa Miller

Give a smouldering look there. The photographer whirs away without a word. He sees the rapport between me and him and takes it in his stride, understanding that this is one of those rare moments when something fantastic can actually happen.

The gods reach down and add their magic in a moment on Earth that's been born out of crass materialism and commercial pressures.

The swimsuits go on and off without effort. The sun moves in its rotation around the earth. The photographer's digital camera fills one card after another with images. The light grip boys sweat profusely in the sun. Hardly anyone makes a sound.

We move like in a cocoon of silence. Changing, trying, shooting. Emoting.

In this moment we, all, create something.

The photo shoot moves to the bedroom.

I have to change quickly and do not even bother to change discreetly any more. The last swimsuit drops to the floor. I stand momentarily naked, completely, then the black lace thong comes on. The transparent bra of matching colour.

It feels like I am still naked. The underwear reveals more than it hides. My nipples stand out through the sheer black lace and my mons is visible so anyone who might want to look closely there.

I sit on the edge of the bed and, my hair now tousled a little, I put my hands on my knees.

Alisa Miller

Back straight, legs slightly apart, I look at the swimsuit I have discarded on the floor.

The camera clicks away feverishly. The photographer is like a wraith, he moves this way and that, his mind all shooting angles.

Inside it's warm. The light grip boys have a harder job. I happen to see one of them. He is lying on his back, on my right. The reflector he is holding carefully angled to light up my breasts. His eyes are locked on my chest. His breathing shallow, fast. His forehead glistening with sweat.

I zone him out. Focus inside, in that place in my mind where everything is happening fast.

People arrive in the room. Leave. It barely registers.

I change again. More shots. The bed feels inviting beneath me. The mattress tells its own story. Firm. Hard. Springy. Expensive. Chosen because of the way it looks.

I stretch this way. Angle my body that way.

The camera clicks.

The day begins to get smaller.

The magic finally ebbs.

I become conscious of the fact that I am lying on my back, one bra strap falling off my shoulder, back arched and hair tousled. Hips thrust forward. The pose is atavistic. It resonates with passion and the kind of mood which makes men and women lose their minds and their senses and enter a world where all that exists is a primal need to connect at a very basic level.

Model

Alisa Miller

Slowly I unwind. My brain disconnects. I come down from my high and become again aware of my immediate surroundings.

"Bravo," soft voice. New. Its owner appears genuine. His eyes, when I see him are filled not with desire but with admiration. "Wrap this up," he turns to address the photographer, suddenly dismissing me from his attention. "We have a two day window to set everything up." He walks out.

There is nothing exceptional about him. Light brown eyes. A frame which appears slight under a light white shirt. Jeans. Trainers. There is a quiet confidence in the way he talks. Moves.

I begin to gather clothes off the bedroom floor. I pick up my own bag so I can get dressed.

"Who was that?" I ask one of the light grip boys that's near the door.

"Sergio, he's the boss."

***

Blink. Time is a very strange thing. We think we understand it because we can measure it. We see its passing in days, weeks, months, years. We have watches that run on caesium atoms which can measure time with the accuracy of a millionth of a second. We know that it is subject to gravity and that those on top of the Empire State Building age a few seconds slower than those at its base. Yet time defies us.

Alisa Miller

It is as much a product of our minds as it is of the universe we live in and its processes.

Blink.

I am sitting at a table for two on a roof garden with a view of the harbour. The play of light on the water makes everything look fantastic and yet I know that in the dark, beyond the reach of my senses other things happen on that water. Cubans swim across the divide between the two countries, fair prey to human predators, sharks, the sea and life itself. Drug dealers ditch monoplanes as the DEA runs its patrol boats. Big game fishermen are preparing for the thrill of big game fishing. And the odd rich man's yacht, stocked with recreational drugs and alcohol floats on the waves, its contents luring young girls starved for money and attention, all too aware of the brief flowering of their youth and eager to make the most of it before time steals it.

Time is the enemy.

Always.

Blink.

"Why did you agree to have dinner with me?" Sergio looks amused and his tone brings me back to the present.

The truth is I do not know. He intrigues me.

"Are you rich?" I ask.

"Moderately,"

"There, you have the answer then," I smile and watch him grin. He is thin and tanned. His body has a tautness which is evident in the way he moves and he dresses in jeans and Ts, unlike any big glossy company boss I have ever seen.

"So you're after my money?"

"Surprised?"

"Relieved," he grins again. "I was really worried you only wanted me for my body."

I laugh. He is funny and he says things in a deadpan way which makes me laugh harder.

"You would not want me wanting you, I am too demanding," I smile.

His talk, joking aside, ranges from the magazine shoot and the promotional material we are putting together to next day's swimwear shot on a boat and the banalities of living in Miami. "Too much sun, too much money and too much sex. This city is drowning in its own excesses."

"Like a modern day Rome,"

"Worse than that, it's like Constantinople before the fall,"

His knowledge of things amazes me. The wine flows and the talk is easy and we suddenly discuss not so much the world as what we want from it. He is older than me by 15 years yet I feel like I am talking to someone with the energy and drive of a teenager and the experience of a grizzled gladiator.

"Your parents were immigrants?" I ask.

"Their parents," he says, "From Serbia, came to America after the second world war and settled here, I am second generation American I guess."

Alisa Miller

Yet he has travelled. Spent a year living rough in Paris before taking off and doing the round of Australia, bumming rides and getting food by working on farms along the way.

"There is a beauty in the world which needs real strength to see. It's like we sleepwalk all the time. We get up, go to work, come home, grab a beer and watch TV and we do this day after day, year after year because the alternative is too painful and requires too much effort. Yet to see the world. To actually be in it and experience it the way it is, is an experience which seers your soul. You realise that people are both desperate and brave. Stupid and good. It is only by realising that the world is a perfect place and that we are only blind to this perfection and really need to try and see it that we begin to understand just how lucky we are."

He talks like this for hours and I listen and as I listen and we drink and he asks my opinion I find myself enjoying the experience in a way which has never happened before.

For a girl sex is a bargaining point. You get to exchange it for companionship, goods, caring, love (sometimes), gifts and friendship. You get to use it to feel less lonely, more wanted and more attractive. Time is always against you in ways a man can never understand. And always you compete with every other girl around you. The ones who are younger appear more appealing, the ones who are older are more experienced. You are constantly under attack.

As a model I am used to the attention of men. As a woman I too make choices which sometimes are good and (most times) bad. After a while I get tired of the one-liners, those who are too glib to be true, those who take you to dinner and expect to sleep with you as a result, or those who simply think because they have money they can buy your body for the night because you hope they will pick you to stay with them.

I became my own woman even if it meant having to spend more nights alone than might be healthy. When I did choose to let myself go the feelings released by my body, the sensations and the passion left me feeling a little betrayed by myself.

I know that I find sex as a handy way to lose myself. My body, trained, pampered and honed to catwalk and photo shoot perfection is always ready to make decisions which I know I will regret in the morning. What I decided long ago was that sex was not going to be a bargaining point for me. It cheapened things way too much for my liking.

This has led to a brutal self honesty which leaves me little room to hide. If I really like someone or if the need to feel sexual release has become more intense than I bear, I have sex. I do it without blaming alcohol, the day or the fact that I thought the person I was with was better or worse than they actually are. It also means that I, each time, know fully well what I am doing and that the consequences might be.

My brain tells me that I just met Sergio that he's an unknown quantity. A guy in charge who likes being in control. Someone who whisked me off to dinner because he likes the way I look and wants to have me.

But I like him. He's unusual. And it's Miami. The city is redolent of decadence.

I know I will probably sleep with him tonight. The knowledge changes nothing outwardly. Under the surface of my skin the story is different. I am aware of the slight moves he makes as he shifts in his chair or turns to talk to the waiter. The whippy sinew of his body is something I find magnetically appealing. I like the fact that unlike almost everyone I have met in Miami the only evidence of money and status he has is the quiet confidence with which he orders food or wine or looks at a place which is evidently expensive. There is no jewellery, no watches, no constantly ringing mobile phone.

You know when the gods have it in for you? I am convinced that they often eavesdrop on our thoughts just so they can piss us off with their next act.

I speak too soon on the phone because the next moment there is a soft chime.

Sergio smoothly palms it from a trouser pocket and listens intently. His expression is blank but in his eyes I can see there is a flash of something fierce. "Ok," he says in a clipped tone. "Hold him there, I will be there in 20," when he puts it down he looks at me and I can see in his expression that he is angry and a little frustrated.

"Trouble?" I ask.

"Maybe. Our entire photographic crew are drunk, stoned, or worse and about to get so out of control that I will have to start looking for new ones tomorrow."

"Is that bad?"

"The schedule is tight and to find new ones now is going to kill our boat photo shoot that's for sure. I need to go." There is deep regret in his voice.

"Where are you going?"

"To get them,"

"Let's go together," it is out before I can stop myself and he looks at me a little surprised. "You promised an adventure," I say.

"They're at Cheetah Hallandale," he says by way of explanation. Those who live in Miami know of Cheetah Hallandale just off I-95. It's a strip club with a reputation where it's 'champagne rooms' often become impromptu scenes of all sorts of improprieties and where the girls perform totally naked in poses and which would not look out of place in a gynaecological examination.

If there is going to be trouble that's the place where it's going to happen.

"I have been there before," I smile, "long story," I do not explain. If he's shocked Sergio does not let on. "I will come with you,"

He is standing up, already motioning for the bill. His face intent as he is assessing the best way to act.

We are outside where his car is already waiting with incredible alacrity. Obviously the restaurant management are used to his having to act quickly.

He is driving a black Porsche Boxster with cream leather bucket seats. I suddenly wonder if he has drunk too much. "I had a glass only," he says and I am stunned both by the fact that he has drunk so little and the ease with which he made it seem like he had drunk more. His honesty now is something I take into account.

There is the squeal of tyre and the sense of acceleration as the car takes to the road and Sergio is focused on navigating Miami traffic.

"Why is this so important?" I am trying to factor in everything, understand more about him and his actions now. There is an urgency which does not make complete sense.

"Ali, I am not quite the boss," he smiles briefly. "I am a coordinator. A consultant, if you like. Rich men with more money than sense hire me to make sure everything which goes on in their project or their little magazine empire or their pointless TV shows goes off without a hitch. This includes bad publicity, police involvement and damaging lawsuits."

Model

Alisa Miller

It makes sense. I understand now that the entire photo crew ending up in jail is going to be bad in more ways than missed schedules.

"And you are discreet?"

"Always," that brief smile again.

The drive is short because he is driving fast. Handling the car like a needle, weaving in and out of lanes of traffic with consummate ease.

"Do you want to stay here?" The Cheetah parking lot is better lit than most but it's no less creepy. Miami often reminds me of the movies where it's featured where the subject is either a serial murderer or a horror killer from another dimension.

"And miss all the fun?"

"Stay behind me. Do not get involved." His tone brooks no argument. I nod.

He comes round to open my door. Makes sure the car is locked.

The bouncer at the door looks like some mutant from another planet, twice the size and height of a normal man. From a distance he reads Sergio's body language and suddenly looks wired and alert, ready for trouble. Then he sees me and, as Sergio approaches, recognises him.

"Mr Tanowicz,"

"Mike,"

"Please come in," there is a momentary pause as he looks at me.

"This is Ali, she's with me Mike. Keep an eye on her if she needs to get out on her own."

"You got it."

We are in. The club is dark, the darkness spiked with strobe lights. The usual mix of sweat, booze and desperate desire in the air and the music is House.

Sergio cuts through the press of bodies like a knife. Polite, firm. Focused. I follow in his wake, quick to leap in before the corridor which he opens up closes again. I brush against people. In the darkness, as I pass, feel a male hand find my ass. Briefly squeeze a buttock. It's that kind of place. I ignore it and move on.

We make it to the main area and Sergio knows the floor manager. I briefly wonder if he comes here but the way he ignores the girls dancing on their stands makes me think this is not his scene. He is here for work.

"Ted, where are they?" he asks the guy in charge. He looks relieved to see Sergio there.

"Thank God you're here Serg, they barricaded the Champagne room,"

"How many?"

"Six,"

"Girls?"

"Four,"

"Any alarms yet?"

"No. But one of your boys is packing," Sergio nods.

"Which way?"

"Level two," the floor manager nods.

The Champagne rooms are what goes for VIP suite at the Cheetah and, depending on the club, they are places where you either get the girls to strip and do almost anything, or places where quite literally, everything goes.

Sergio takes the steps two at a time, gets to the door, quickly checks left and right to see who is looking and then, with a fluid movement which speaks of suppressed, controlled, physical power, spins on one foot, kicks out backwards with his other. There is the crunch of splintering wood and the door flies open with a crunch and he is in.

I am a few steps back, still trying to compute what I just saw. I squeeze in through the wreckage of the door itself and the scene inside is almost straight out of a film. There are red leather couches and cushions everywhere. Six champagne bottles, at half empty on the table in the middle. All the girls are completely naked.

One is on the far couch. On all fours. She has a guy in her mouth and one of the light grip boys is holding onto her hips from behind. His own hips a blur as he pumps into her. There are shed clothes everywhere. All the girls are completely naked. The guys are in various stages of undress.

A couple of girls are on their knees, on the floor. Their heads alternating between two guys lying on one of the leather couches

The tableau is hypnotic. It has the quality of the unexpected and yet strangely familiar. It shocks the senses not so much by what it shows but by the fact that you see people you associate with suddenly engaged in an act of total intimacy with total strangers they have bought.

Alisa Miller

I make sure my back is against a wall and I am out of the way.

Sergio is amongst them really fast. He makes for two guys who have a girl tied down. Her hands bound behind her back with her own bra. They are busy inserting a champagne bottle in her and as she cries out one of them slaps her. I do not hear the slap. I see the man who slapped her, eyes glazed with alcohol and something else, raise his hand again. Then Sergio is there. The slap never reaches the girl's face, pressed down against the leather of the cushion.

Sergio grabs the man's wrist, pulls against the elbow locking he joint and unbalancing him. I watch in shock and a rising feeling of admiration. He moves like an artist. The man is locked down, Sergio slaps him across the face, hard, whispers something urgently to him, sees he is not getting through and then, almost gently taps him with a hook on the side of the jaw. Cradles his head so he does not hit the floor hard as he drops.

Five left.

The one who was busy inserting the champagne bottle in the girl comes off her angrily. He is fully dressed, his fly undone. He is holding the champagne bottle like a club, fails to recognise Sergio, tries to come at him. His other hand tagging at something in his pocket.

Sergio recognises the handle of the gun before me. Sees that it is momentarily tangled up, the fact that the man is doing two things at the same time, unbalancing him and with surgical precision turns his body and kicks in a textbook-perfect side kick into the man's solar plexus.

There is a momentary gasp as the man's eyes go wide open, threatening to pop out of their sockets. His body goes into shock and his brain is suddenly gasping to get the oxygen he needs. He falls, like he's been poleaxed, a bundle of heaving flesh on the floor.

Sergio bends, extracts the gun and quickly pockets it. Turns to the rest who are just now coming up hands tagging at clothing.

"What the hell do you think you're doing?' he yells and his voice cuts like ice through their drunkenness. "We have a shoot tomorrow. There are models flying in and we have two boats and crew booked and you do this?" he motions with the flat of his hand. He is, I can see, on the balls of his feet, balancing lightly, suddenly ready to spring into instant action. His hands already in front of him, open, seemingly friendly, within striking distance of these boozed up boys.

He makes it look easy. Years of kick-boxing tell me it's not.

Sergio, motions to the girls. "Get out of here. I will speak to Ted. You have the rest of the night off on me." He says. They quickly untie their bound friend, grab their clothes, step into gold hot pants, boots. Skip out of there, dazed and unsure of what has just happened.

I reflect briefly on how easy it is for things to get out of control. At some point in the evening an invisible line was crossed and what would be fun for the guys and work for the girls turned into something else entirely. Money and alcohol are a bad combination.

Sergio moves like a one-man clean-up squad. He bullies and intimidates with his tone, body language and expressions. His voice is tight with anger and studied fury. He gets through to them in minutes. Stops things from getting out of hand. Watches imperiously as the guys pick up their unconscious friend off the floor.

"We'll discuss this tomorrow at the photo shoot, before we start," he says, and the expression on their eyes is that of condemned men hearing their sentence. "I'll have taxies come to pick you up. You're going back to your hotel tonight. The evening's over."

I watch like a shadow, following the group, staying close to Sergio, as he talks to the floor manager. One more man. Says something to one of the girls who had been in the Champagne room. From one pocket he takes out a wad of cash, passes it to the floor manager. The guy nods. Agrees with everything Sergio says.

He then goes to the girls who are in one corner as a small group, huddled away from the music, barely realizing what had happened, how close things came to getting totally out of control.

He talks to them. Reaches into a pocket again. It is too dark to see but I guess more money is passed around.

Model

Alisa Miller

I sign inwardly. Miami. It would be hypocritical to say the whole town runs on money like it's some kind of judgement. The whole world is like that. Miami is probably a little more honest and a little less hypocritical than most places.

"Hello there," slightly slurred voice behind me makes me turn and I am looking at a drunk customer. He is dressed in the required light suit and blue open neck shirt of the professional and his body looks like an athlete going to seed. "You're on your own here pretty lady?"

"No," I smile and edge a little further away.

"Oh, really?"

"Yes, really."

"Who you're with then pretty lady?"

I inwardly sigh. Men! "See that guy over there?" I point to Sergio, "I am with him."

The guy squints. Sees Sergio. At that precise moment Sergio looks over. Nods at me. Then sees the man standing a little further behind me. Makes a curt, chopping motion with the flat of one hand.

I see it. Turn around to see what the man's response is but he is no longer there. He is gone.

Impressive. Intriguing.

It takes ten more minutes before we can head back out to the parking lot where the Porsche is parked.

***

Blink. Time has its own momentum. Sergio has a condo in Brickell Keys, in a gated community which has hi-tech laser tags for entry keys. The view of the sea is breath taking and, according to Sergio, the sunrise is world class.

He has a glass in his hand. "You want some?" he asks and his tone is casual. Relaxed.

"What is it?"

"Kinclaith, a single malt,"

"Whisky?"

"Technically yes. I suppose. It's aged in casks over 36 years and shipped here from Scotland. It tastes a little like heaven but I suppose you could call it a whisky,"

His deadpan voice makes me smile. "You were cool out there tonight," I say.

"It almost got out of hand," he says and there is a tightness in his voice.

"It didn't. You had some impressive moves." He nods. "Seriously,"

"I have been training since I was 13 he says,"

"What in?"

"Tae Kwon Do – used to be US champion in my weight division,"

"Impressive,"

"It's much better if things had not got to that stage."

"You handled it," I say.

He takes a sip from his glass and walks away.

Model

Alisa Miller

"Is everything ok?"

"Yeah, I had better get you a cab,"

I am a little puzzled. It's not the kind of response I am used to when I am alone with a guy in his condo. "Why not get me a drink instead?"

He stops his pacing and looks at me. "You're sure?"

"I asked,"

"I know but here's the thing. It's late and I am really hyped. The action at the Cheetah has made me edgy and this," he jiggles the whisky, "is how I am dealing with it. You're here with me and I find you fascinating, beautiful, intelligent and with a very unique view on life. Normally I'd want you in my bed but we both know that in a week you will move on to another photo shoot and really you are too intelligent to be another notch in a wired guy's bed post," he gives me his brief grin and sips his whisky again.

It is, admittedly, the best turn down I could have ever imagined.

"So you'd rather not get me a whisky too?"

"If we both start on the whisky this will end up on my bed,"

"Why not the floor?"

My remark makes him smile. "Whisky it is for the lady then," he says.

Blink. Time has its own way of flowing. I feel the sensation of cool night air on my skin. The balcony doors are open and the day's Miami heat has dissipated into the coolness of the night.

My clothes are somewhere on the living room floor. Sergio's body feels hot and taut.

When you let it sex has a way of connecting in your mind in pathways which take you to a totally different place.

I feel his lips tracing a line down my neck, reaching my breasts, my nipples are on fire. His mouth quenches it.

Blink. Disjointed time.

I lose myself in something unreal.

Sergio's hips thrust urgently against me. He groans when my long nails rake his back.

Despite the long day he is tireless. The minutes stretch into hours. Exhaustion and exhilaration, urgency and need, overtake us both. When he comes for the last time, his semen this time flowing across my breasts, I sense the last of his energy is spent.

He falls on the rumpled black satin sheets next to me.

His hand reaches out and his fingertips touch mine.

Neither of us talks. We lie there breathing heavily, feeling our limbs slowly turn to led as fatigue and satiation play their part and sleep finally conquers us. The magic which has so unexpectedly happened cocoons us in its shared moment and we drift off to sleep like a couple who have known each other for centuries.

#16

Brickell Keys, Miami.

The day after the night before is always a little awkward the first time. My body aches, inside, where Sergio had been the night before. I shift my legs slightly across the bed, remember the wildness and wanton which has happened. Cherish the moment and the memory.

The sun is coming through the vertical venetian blinds. Its bars fall across Sergio's lean frame and give me the time to study it. He is lean, like a dancer. His muscles flat and hard. His hair dark, face angular. There are faint scars across one shoulder. His stomach is flat, muscled hard with the ribbed look of the trained six pack.

I recall how he felt. The way his body spasmed as I made him come. His hands and mouth on me felt wildly exciting and comfortingly familiar at the same time.

This man is a mystery I say to myself. Yet, for the first time in a very long time I wake up in a strange place, in a strange bed and feel totally at peace with myself.

I pad slowly out of bed not bothering with clothes. The sensation feels liberating.

His condo, like him, has that mix between functionality and aesthetics. I open the kitchen cupboards, pick out what I need. The fridge provides eggs, milk, some herbs are in a drawer and there are fresh tomatoes and basil. The coffee is Colombian and I put the filter machine on.

Out of the big bay windows the ocean is beginning to come to life and the sun, rising slowly out of the horizon feels suddenly so primal and so beautiful that it makes the breath catch in my throat and tears come to my eyes. To see such beauty in the world, so unexpectedly, to feel part of this planet. I sometimes feel I do not deserve it.

"Morning,"

Sergio's voice startles me and I almost drop the eggs I am holding. He is standing by the doorway to the open plan living room/kitchen and he too is naked. He smiles. "Breakfast?" he says and pads towards me with a feline grace.

"Omelette OK?" I ask.

He comes round the breakfast bar to me. Stands behind me and I can feel he is erect, pressing against the small of my back. He puts his arms around me and gently eases the eggs out of my hand. "You," he breathes against my ear.

His hands cup and squeeze my breasts. I arch my body against his.

We have, somehow, made it to the living room. The space crossed from the kitchen counter in a way which has both escaped us. He bends me over a leather armchair and I feel his hands cupping my buttocks, prizing them apart and then he is deep inside of me.

Model

Alisa Miller

I gasp.

The morning sun's rays play on us. What happens is primal. We lose part of our humanity. Gain a shared experience which transcends words.

Later, much later, it is he who makes breakfast and brings it to me. We eat on the floor, plates and glasses of orange juice between us as the sun walks across the room.

"What do we do now?" he asks.

I know what he means. Sometimes, something happens which changes anything. I know the last thing I want is to pack my bags and say goodbye to this man.

"Elope?" I suggest.

He laughs. Rolls on his back on the floor. I marvel at the ease with which he displays his body.

"I need three days to wrap this up and you have a shoot later today,"

"I know,"

"Why don't we have dinner tonight?"

"You'll pick me up?"

"No. I'll have your things brought over. I do not want to miss you for a second more than I need to."

I reach across and kiss him on the lips. He wraps a strong arm around my waist and lifts me onto him, my body pressed completely against his.

"Nice way to start the day," he breathes against my lips.

I am too busy exploring his body with my hands and mouth to answer meaningfully.

***

Blink. Time is the enemy. It flows too fast. I am on the terrace, sitting cross-legged, naked beneath a thin white chemise and as the sun's first rays hit the Earth I know my body's outline is clearly visible to Sergio sitting in the room behind me and looking out through the open balcony door.

I close my eyes, blind myself to the beauty of the world.

My mind floats in darkness.

My body ceases to exist.

"Ali," words from the night before. "Why don't you stay?" Sergio's voice is tight with pain. Sweat beads our naked bodies. The memory of his fresh upon mine.

Time is running out. Where have the minutes gone?

I am going to try and explain the way I live my life. I believe, firmly, in the moment and its power. In the ability of the events which have gone before to become a sum the weight of which drives us onto the next step and the step after that and the one after that so that in hindsight things become inevitable and seem obvious.

My own sense of fatalism. The fact that I have seen premature death and stunning beauty walk hand-in-hand so many times, my training as a psychologist and my own beliefs regarding life and its trajectory combine into a seamless whole. I make decisions using the best information I have available and balance them against the way they make me feel.

If I had information which led me to believe, for instance, that the killing of a single person might save a million others I would then need to balance it against my own sense of how this action would make me feel before I decide. If something does not sit well with me, no matter how much logic dictates it should be done, I will not do it. But I never allow emotion to completely rule my every action. Logic is my first recourse.

In my mind right now I am in total darkness.

The rising sun's rays caress my face and the slight breeze coming from the sea, even this high, smells of salt and the romanticism of centuries. The sunlight turns my chemise transparent.

I float in darkness examining the way I feel. To stay with Sergio is not difficult. I find his way of thinking and working fascinating and I love the way he makes me feel. But modelling is a hard career. There is travel involved. The attention of men away from your partner and everything this engenders, plus the degree of insecurity any man going out with a model who attracts attention the moment they step out of the house, inevitably feels.

You would think that we live in modern times now, these things do not matter, but they do. It was a lesson I learnt with Ray the hard way.

Giving up my independence is not a solution either. All my life I have been my own woman. I cannot change that, nor do I want to.

Modelling is not all I do. Not any more. My contract with Carlos is in hand. Neil has sent a copy to my Blackberry and I spent an hour the night before going through it.

I have been working on notes, putting a book together. Using my experience from counselling sessions plus what I see as a woman, as a model. Writing I can do from anywhere. I do not need to travel for that, nor do I need to be in Britain.

There is a part of me which feels a deep, persistent sadness each time I see people miserable because of a relationship, or their inability to form one. In counselling sessions I have been stunned by the fact that, many times, couples find themselves so caught up in their own personal issues that they cannot see the obvious solution lying in front of them for their relationship to develop.

I've learnt the fact that even the best of personal intentions can be lost in translation as couples fail to communicate with each other.

I reach a decision, deep inside me.

I slowly stand up and walk back inside the condo. Sergio has been sitting in an armchair watching me. He is only wearing shorts and the sight of his lean body fills me with desire but I fight the urge down. More important things than sex are being decided right now. He watches me approach him, his eyes drinking me in, itemising my outline.

"Ali," he breathes.

For a few moments we say nothing else.

He stands up and puts his arms around me. I feel his body pressed tightly against me own and as his hands travel down my back I can feel the sudden male response against the flatness of my belly. He buries his face in my hair and takes a deep breath, drinking in my scent.

"Serg," I begin but he places a finger against my lips silencing me. We part and momentarily stare at each other.

"You know," he says, "all this," he throws an arm to encompass the condo and its view outside, "means nothing without you. Suppose I give it all up. Follow you."

"Why would you do that?"

"I love you,"

There. Three words which can stop a girl's heart. It's so simple and yet so complicated. I stop him from saying anything else. "Don't," I whisper into his lips.

He kisses me.

"I really don't care. I can give all this up for you. I will find something else to do."

Insanity. We barely know each other. Yet it feels so right.

"I'll give up modelling," my lips flutter against his own.

The stiffening of his body tells me he has understood. "Ali, no! You love modelling,"

"Time to move on. It's been a long five years."

"Ali!"

"There are other things I can do,"

"What?"

"I have been wanting to write a book for some time. Maybe something which can help others. The publisher's contract came through last night. "

"A book?"

"Yeah, you know, black squiggles on white paper."

He laughs and his lips close the gap, find mine. His tongue insistent. And I feel his arms wrap around me. His hands finding and cupping my naked buttocks, under the chemise. He is hard. I can feel him pressed against me and he lifts me in his arms.

The sensation is perfect because I can feel the world recede. Cares dropping off me like petals off a flower and I know, in that instant, that moment, that the decision I made was right. That the years of loneliness and pain have melted away.

I have finally come home.

- The End -

ABOUT THE AUTHOR

Alisa Miller, has lived in three countries and two continents. A former model she has used her training to focus on relationship issues and her first book, 'Ultimate Guide to the Perfect Relationship' became an internet phenomenon appearing both as an eBook and on paper all over the web in the first week of publication. She has, since, written for hundreds of websites and magazines. She edited a magazine and has been working hard on more books in the dating, sex and relationships areas. She runs her own website and spends more time online than even she admits is healthy.

Other books by the same author

Alisa Miller's books are available to buy from every major bookstore on both sides of the Atlantic. They can be bought online at Amazon.com plus a large number of established online book retailers.

They are also available as downloads for Amazon Kindle, the Sony eBook reader and smartphones and PDAs from

Mobipocket.com and any large online eBook retailer.

Stay current

The author is active in the content of her own website which is updated on an almost daily basis. Apart from articles on relationships, real-life stories and the author's own Blog her website: www.alisa-miller.com is also the place where you can find her latest publications at a discounted price.

KEEP IN TOUCH

Alisa Miller maintains a Facebook Fan page where she interacts with her fans regularly and messages all those who join once a week:

To join the author's fan page go to:
http://www.facebook.com/Miller.Alisa

Model

Alisa Miller

Model

Alisa Miller

www.ingramcontent.com/pod-product-compliance
Lightning Source LLC
Chambersburg PA
CBHW070015260626
47159CB00005B/1818